RED WALLS

CHRISTINA BERGLING

Published by Dead Fox Publishing
deadfoxpub.com

Editing: Poppy McDonald & Kelley York
Cover illustration: B.C. Maxwell at IlluMax
Cover typography & design: Kelley York
Interior graphics: Kelley York
Interior Formatting: Kelley York

Digital 978-1-960322-22-7
Paperback 978-1-960322-23-4
Hardcover 978-1-960322-24-1

DEAD FOX
PUBLISHING

CONTENT NOTES

Please note: it should be assumed that basic horror tropes will apply. These include death, gore, and violence.

ONE

SATURDAY 1:11 A.M.

BLOOD TRICKLED FROM Talia's nose, drying at the top of her lip. Beneath the screaming static of her nerves, she didn't notice it. Her face could have fallen off for all she cared. She felt raw and exposed, a bloodied skeleton staggering down the asphalt. With the adrenaline draining from her, the pain surfaced. As much as she needed to get home, as much as it had been her only thought these past hours, her muscles struggled to deliver her this final stretch.

The quiet of the neighborhood unnerved her. Dawn threatened the edge of the dark, and the air contracted around its approach. No one else moved on the streets or outside their houses. The wind barely whispered through the towering trees in clipped yards. She heard no cars rolling nearby. Suburbia slumbered. The area felt abandoned or asleep, as if everyone had moved on without her, as if the world had napped through her assault.

She pinched her lips between her teeth. *Fitting, since no one will ever know.*

She scraped to a stop when her house came into view. At the sight of it—*home*—tears sprang back into her eyes. It felt impossible, surreal, like a mirage.

Home. I never thought I would see it again.

She pictured her mother and father inside. Her mother would be seething over the missed call, pacing around the house through her worry. Her father would be perched on the edge of the couch cushion, attempting to talk her mother down.

Shit.

She needed to get herself together. She needed a story. What had happened to her tonight?

Taking a deep breath, she shook her hands at her side. Under the nearest streetlight, she looked down to survey her appearance.

"Fuck," she exhaled at the sight.

Her trembling fingers brushed over her wrinkled shirt. The hem lifted to expose the scratches drawn down her stomach. The button of her jeans was torn away, leaving the waistband of her pants wilted open. Leaves and grass clung to her clothes, obscuring the minute droplets of blood. In the dim light, she brushed until the fabric burned at her palms. She tugged her pants up and shirt down to cover her belly and ripped button.

She smoothed over and over until her injuries lost feeling and the gesture lost meaning. Then her hands migrated to her cheeks, and she swiped gentler at the tear tracks. Holding her own face, she stared at her house through splayed fingers.

Her nerves clamored for attention, a symphony of injuries sending screaming messages to her brain. She could not see herself. She could not feel anything beyond the pain in her face. So, she did not wipe the blood from her nose.

Not her first mistake of the night.

A part of her felt hollowed out, stolen, missing. There was an aching vacancy beneath the hand clutching her stomach. Most of her other injuries were internal, hidden. So, her parents didn't have to know. They didn't have to know how close they came to losing another daughter. They couldn't know. If they did, she knew what they would do.

As she stumbled past the low shrubs her father meticulously clipped, the crimson dribble remained on her lip like a blinking sign. The toes of her shoes dragged on the driveway where she'd learned how to ride a bike. It was all she could do to cling to herself and trudge to the front door.

TWO
SATURDAY 1:17 A.M.

AUTUMN STOOD AT the massive granite kitchen island with her heart battering her ribs. As she drummed her fingers, muscles flexed under her brown skin. Her thick curls were bound atop her head, branching out to stand wild. She hovered in front of her chair, unable to sit, unable to hold still. An untouched coffee mug cooled before her. Her mind scrolled through a million disastrous endings to this night, and her body twitched against each of them.

Nothing was okay, nothing could be okay, until she knew where her daughter was. She could not quiet until she felt her child with her own hands.

She attempted to soothe the tide of anxiety, pacify it with rational thoughts. Instead, she swayed with its current. Its undertow wrapped around her, threatening to pull her under. In her mind, it was a snowy night years ago. A white sheet over a small bloody hand.

Ballet class. Icy road. Broken glass. A tiny, pink coffin surrounded by white lilies.

Not again. Not again. Not again. The thought circled like a prayer, as if denial was enough to move the world.

Colin sank into the chair beside her, wrapped around his own cold coffee. His pale, bald head shined in the hanging light. He stared into the placid liquid, reaching up periodically to trace his palm down her back. Though it failed to soothe her shuffling. She wanted to let him comfort her, but his gestures were maddening pacifications until she knew for sure. She could not look at him and see the shared fear on his face, the looming grave in his eyes.

The front door latch clicked, and they both startled. The storm in Autumn's mind solidified and slid down her spine like ice, shedding all the what-ifs and worst-case scenarios. Only a live child could walk through the door tragically late.

Colin rose beside her, fingers already tugging at the blonde, wiry ends of his beard. She stopped breathing, legs tensed to launch her across the room.

The door parted just enough for Talia to slink around. She slithered through the opening and crouched, as if it were possible to sneak in unnoticed. As if they had not been waiting for her for hours. She should have known they would be right here, had been right here since she missed curfew and didn't answer her phone.

Autumn surged forward, her entire body a flood of electric impulse. Talia was so much more alive than the dead, broken phantom in Autumn's anxiety. It took Autumn the breadth of the living room to clock blood on her daughter's face, dirty and disheveled clothes, fuzzy hair.

Blood. On her daughter's face.

She seized Talia. Her child was alive, in her hands. She could touch her. But someone had done this to her. Someone had hurt her. A burning blend of relief and anger and worry doused her, leaving her nerves crackling. Impulses to care collided with instincts to protect, turning into a blur of urges. Her hands trembled as she moved them over Talia.

Colin chased her. As Autumn examined their child, he tugged at his long beard, the hairs snapping back at release.

"What happened?" Autumn asked, gripping Talia's cheeks to scrutinize her face. The entire room faded around her, even Colin. It was just her and Talia's impending answer. How could she fix it? Who did she have to go after?

Talia stared, dazed. She touched the blood then squinted at her fingertips. "It's just a bloody nose, Ma." She tried to lean away, but Autumn held her tight.

Talia hesitated too long. Autumn could hear the lie in the quiet space between. In that micro-second, the torrent of possibilities resurged in her. She chomped her tongue to keep it silent. She needed to be calm, soothing, and receptive to get answers. Then she could decide what to do with them.

She had to tip her daughter's face down, just a little, to look at her. When had Talia gotten taller than her? The blood on her face and that emptiness, new in her eyes, made her look older. Shoving down the crawling sensations in her chest, Autumn focused on the blood.

"What happened, Tal?" Colin said beside them. He took another step closer, looking down at both of them.

Talia opened her mouth then buttoned her lips. The skin puckered at the pressure, and tears flooded her eyes. Pinning her arms around her chest, she pulled away from her parents, choking on an ugly, sloppy cry.

The sound broke Autumn's heart. She melted, diffused in the steam of her rage. She drew Talia into a tender embrace. Immediately, with her child in her arms, warmth flooded over her nerves. The control of feeling her breathing and knowing she was safe.

Talia was rigid against her at first, stiff and quivering with her cries. Autumn stroked her fluffy curls down as she poured hushed comforts into her ear. She filled her lungs enough to stretch her ribs into Talia then exhaled slow, encouraging her daughter to breathe deep with her, like how she used to after a skinned knee or bruised heart.

Talia relented and wound her hands into the back of Autumn's shirt. Autumn clutched her, as she had since she was an infant, folding her daughter against her body in the way she still fit perfectly. She wanted to hold her forever; she wanted to go burn down the world that did this.

"I got you, LiLi," Autumn cooed, looking up to Colin with a steeled gaze, venting her smoldering anger. "You are safe here. Dad and I will keep you safe." The last words hardened like a promise.

After the sobs quelled, Talia finally raised her face. The blood from her nose smeared across Autumn's shirt, but no one cared. Colin exhaled deep into Autumn's hair. His arm snaked silent and supportive up her back. The other found Talia's shoulder, creating a circle around them.

Autumn knew the language. *I'm here. I'll be here for you.*

"You're not in trouble, Tal, no matter what happened." Colin spoke slow and heavy, the way he talked to her when she was very young, making sure she registered every word. "No secrets, no lies in this house. Just tell us what happened."

Autumn kept running soothing hands over Talia's back, the gesture becoming compulsive. She tried to focus on her child in front of her, yet she stiffened with each swipe of her own hand. Colin gave her a gentle squeeze at her hip to remind her he was there, to ground her back in the moment.

Talia's bottom lip quivered. She looked between her parents, helpless. That look in her eyes, the change in her face hit Autumn somewhere deep, somewhere primal and maternal. She didn't need words to register the significance. She found resolve in what Talia did not say and knew what she needed to do.

"Why don't I help you get cleaned up?" Autumn gathered Talia's hands. "Get that blood off your face. Get you out of these dirty clothes."

Colin released them, gaping at her words, his eyes narrowing. Autumn flashed him a firm expression as she guided Talia. He raised a finger.

"What if we need to…" he trailed off.

Something flared in Autumn. She froze and stared back, pushing out her lips. "Need to what?" she asked.

"What if we need to call the cops?" Colin near-whispered. "What if we need to—I don't know—preserve the evidence?" He moved his hand with his words before releasing it.

Echoes of her own screams filled Autumn's ears, swelling to deafen her. She held herself against the flinch. She blinked against the red and blue lights flickering along shattered glass and twisted metal, off the metal badge in her way, the hand on the butt of a service gun.

Calm down, ma'am. Have you been drinking? Take anything? Words Colin had not heard. Words that would have never been said to him.

Autumn closed her eyes for a breath, banishing the past from her mind, as she drew Talia into her. She did not have time to be irritated at him; her child needed her.

When she looked at him, the hard look on her face changed, adopted a vicious edge. She let her hard, copper eyes speak for her. Colin pulled his lips into his mouth and bit into them, his face flushing as a vein threatened at his temple. Talia furrowed her brow as she glanced between the two, the unspoken exchange moving between her parents.

Autumn guided Talia upstairs. Her nerves twitched as she placed light fingertips on the girl's back. Every inch of her skin bristled and writhed as she forced her footfalls to be slow and gentle, not slamming in the anger she felt, not rushing her wounded child. She kept her breaths tempered up the staircase that suddenly felt never-ending.

This was her purpose in this moment: to mother. She knew what she would do in the moments after.

When they shuffled into the small, white, porcelain space, Autumn pressed the door closed behind them. A relief to be alone with her daughter, to selfishly control her care. The counter stretched along the wall, littered with Talia's toothbrush, toothpaste, a brush, a comb, a scatter of rubber bands. A mess that usually would send irritation tightening over Autumn's skin. She didn't even see it. She moved to the bathtub; the oversized rectangle that had been half the reason she liked this house. Bending over, she released the water from the faucet, steam immediately crawling up from the thrashing water.

"A bath?" Talia asked, her voice small.

Autumn nodded and hummed as she sprinkled Epsom salt and bubble solution into the water. Bubbles bloomed on the shaking surface of the bath.

"I haven't taken a bath in years." The teenage tone edged Talia's words.

Autumn ignored the flinch at the flare of attitude. "It will help." She placed her hands on her daughter's shoulders. "Can I help you get in?"

Talia's arms climbed around her waist, and her eyes slid away. "Aren't I too old to be helped bathe?"

Autumn smiled, releasing a laughing breath. "I wasn't too old when Grandmama helped me on and off the toilet after giving birth." She shifted a hand to Talia's cheek. "You are never too old for my help, LiLi. If you want it."

Talia nodded, her brown curls bobbing. "Do you miss Grandmama?"

"Almost as much as I miss Juni." Autumn's smile faltered before she spread it farther across her lips.

Stepping back, she gauged Talia's face. Grasping the hem of her shirt, she tugged it over her head. The motion kicked her back to the thousand times she had done it with a much smaller Talia and much smaller shirts. The flash sliced through her, and she had to stop breathing to hold her expression steady.

Talia wilted from the shirt, collapsing down to cradle herself. Autumn swept her eyes over her child, making sure not to stare, making sure not to hesitate. The pouring water continued to pound beside them. The sound filled the bathroom, hugging them.

Purple bruises blossomed on Talia's caramel skin. Autumn noticed the grip marks near her wrists, the scrapes across her palms first as Talia slipped her arms from the shirt sleeves. Running soothing fingers down Talia's arms, she acted as if she had seen nothing. When Autumn reached for Talia's jeans, she saw the button had been torn free, and the zipper clung desperately to stay up. Above the waist of the pants, scratches and more bruises spread over Talia's belly.

Talia caught her mother's eyeline and flinched back, gasping. Autumn hushed her softly yet remained where she stood as Talia slid from her pants and remaining clothes. Autumn extended her hand and helped steady Talia into the tub. As Talia lowered into the steaming water, Autumn crouched down to turn off the faucet.

Before Talia could hide below the blanket of bubbles, Autumn glimpsed the bright, swollen wound low on one side of her stomach. An angry, red line carved across her daughter's flesh—a burn maybe—surrounded by sympathetic purples and deeper browns.

Then it was gone below the surface, and Autumn looked away to blink back raging tears. The anger would come next.

"How does that feel?" Autumn asked, pretending to rifle through product bottles.

"Better."

"Get your hair wet, and I will condition it for you."

"You haven't washed my hair in a bath since I was a kid." Talia pulled a mound of bubbles toward her face.

"We wouldn't have to wash your hair so often if you let me braid it." Tears choked back; Autumn turned to Talia. She gathered the conditioner tub into her hand.

"My hair isn't coarse enough to keep braided. It just gets fuzzy."

"It wouldn't get fuzzy if you used the jojoba oil."

Talia rested her head against the side of the tub and glared at her mother. "Is this really what you want to talk about right now?"

"No." Autumn looked to the conditioner in her hands and unscrewed the lid. "I want to talk about what happened tonight."

Dipping her fingers into the mixture, she pulled out a dollop. She worked through Talia's wet hair, massaging the conditioner from her scalp down to the ends, then reached for the wide-tooth comb and brought it through the curls in slow, rhythmic strokes.

Autumn watched her own hands as she worked, mesmerized by the repetitive gestures, lost in a tangle of memories of her mother's hands on her own head and her hands in Talia and Juniper's hair when they were small. The moment became meditative, even as the tingle of tears wriggled along her sinuses.

In the hallway, a floorboard whined softly. Colin on the other side of the door. She could practically feel his fingertips flirting with the doorknob. His objections were a roar in the back of her mind. She willed him away. She silently begged for this moment with her daughter. The floorboard squeaked again before soft footfalls retreated back downstairs.

Talia left her head against the side of the tub. She slithered a hand up to support her face against the white basin. When Autumn looked down at her face, a tear slipped down her daughter's cheek.

"LiLi," Autumn said.

Talia swiped at the tear and pressed back. The bubbles popped and dispersed as she gathered herself at the back of the tub. Her knees surfaced, and she drew them into her body. More fat tears swelled in her eyes.

"Mama," she managed.

Autumn pressed her body against the dry side of the tub, leaving a hand on the rim, available if Talia wanted it. Then she waited.

"I can't," Talia finally said. The cries strangled her words. Her face contorted around them. Then she wrangled her features still. "I'm fine," she choked. "Nothing happened. I just fell. I was—" She averted her eyes to the basin. "I was drunk and I fell."

She stole a glimpse at her mother and gripped her knees tighter, as if to ball herself up and disappear beneath the water. Autumn's mind whirred. She didn't give a shit about Talia drinking. Not in this moment. But she wanted to scream at her daughter and shake the truth from her. Why wouldn't she just tell her? Why couldn't she just say it? Autumn thought she was the type of mom Talia could talk to. At least, that's what she had always told herself after she recovered from Juni.

"Where were you?" She spoke slowly to keep her voice level. Her stomach threatened to froth up to her molars.

"House party."

"Where?"

"Other side of the woods."

"Did something happen there? Did someone hurt you?"

Talia shrank a little more. "Nothing happened at the party. I just drank too much. I fell walking home."

Autumn clung to the tub to steady herself. Rage took the white of the basin and the walls and burned out her sight entirely.

Ripped jeans, restraint bruises, adamant denial.

Autumn knew what these signs meant, and she now wanted to vomit it on the floor to get it out of her. Was it the party? Had some guy, some group of boys, hurt her baby? Where would she find them now?

"Ma?" Talia called.

The bathroom snapped into focus around Autumn. Grip trembling, her entire forearm quaked. She glanced at it, as if it were another person's shaking arm, then drew it back to her body. Taking a deep breath, she looked at Talia.

"Talia." Autumn kept her voice deadly calm. "We both know something happened."

"No, nothing—"

Autumn's face silenced her daughter. "Tell me which house."

Talia shot up in the water, splashing her mother. Autumn did not notice. "Nothing happened at the party. I promise!"

"Then what?"

Talia chewed her lip. "I fell on Monere Lane. These people, the ones who live in Red Walls House, they…" She abandoned the words.

Autumn could scarcely contain herself. She quivered in the effort to compose herself. "Talia." She rooted herself in her daughter's name. She let her hardened expression, the mom face she had given thousands of times, speak for her.

"Ma, you don't understand." Talia's eyes widened. "You can't go—" She steadied herself again. "Nothing happened. You don't have to do anything. Really."

The more Talia lied, the more she didn't say, the sharper Autumn's assumptions became. She did not need words; Talia's injuries had told enough of the story. The spaces between her words said the rest. Red Walls House. She knew where she was going. That's all she really needed to know, so she forced herself to still. Shaking her head, she gathered Talia's hand, coaxing her back into the bubbles.

"I will take care of it." Autumn kept Talia's hand and stroked her fingers along the back of it.

"Please, don't, Ma. I don't want you doing what you wanted to after Juni."

Autumn gulped and looked down at Talia's hand. "Like I should have for Juni."

"Ma," Talia breathed. "That was an accident."

"It is not an accident when someone is drunk." The tears escaped Autumn's eyes. She swept them away before they could reach her cheeks. Then she leveled her gaze at her daughter. "Is this really what you want to talk about right now?"

They never wanted to talk about that night.

Talia shook her head and slid deeper into the water. Releasing her daughter's hand, Autumn brought her chin to rest on the edge of the tub. Talia's face had changed, softened by treading on that tender wound from the past. They stared at each other for a long, silent moment.

"Promise me," Talia finally said. "Promise me you won't."

"I promise," Autumn lied without a twitch.

After the water disappeared down the drain, Autumn wrapped Talia in her robe. Talia slipped her pajamas on over her bruises and wounds while Autumn pretended not to squint after the injuries. Then Autumn twisted loose braids into Talia's hair. She guided Talia to her bed and tucked the blankets snuggly around her, as if she were still a kid.

Talia sank into the pillow, lifting her copper eyes to her mother. Her eyelids were thick, puffed and swollen from all the tears. Autumn pressed her palm to Talia's forehead like a sick child.

"Do you want anything?" Autumn asked.

"Can I just have some water?"

"Of course, LiLi." She patted at Talia's knee through the blanket. "What if I called Willow and Ricky over?"

Talia's brow furrowed. "It's real late."

"Do you think they'll care?"

"No."

"Would it make you feel better to talk to them?"

Talia sank deeper into the bed as she nodded.

Autumn padded from the room and down the stairs. The carpet suddenly felt too soft, threatening to suck her down to drown in the thrashing sea of her emotions. She heaved as she clutched the railing. She didn't know if it was cold relief pouring over her or molten rage. Or both.

Colin waited for her, frozen rigid on the couch. He wrung his hands over his knees, tugging then releasing his pant legs. When Autumn landed on the hardwood floor, his pale irises flashed.

"You didn't," he breathed. Disappointment weighed his words.

She met his eyes, marching past him into the kitchen. He launched from the cushion to pursue her.

"Autumn," he pressed.

"Didn't what?" She snatched a glass from the cabinet and moved to the sink.

He stepped into her way. "You didn't wash away all that evidence."

Pursing her lips tight, she squared toward him. "Evidence for what?"

"Evidence of what happened to our daughter. Evidence for the police." He pressed his hip against the counter and gestured wildly.

She shoved a thick breath out of her nose and closed her eyes. When she opened them, they had solidified again. He held firm.

"After Juni," she said, biting at her lip and shaking her head. "After my father." She brought that sharp gaze back to him. "I know you did not say *police* to me again."

The red and blue lights in her memory threatened to blind her. They flashed brighter and faster with her anger. His words, his pale ignorance, pushed her away.

Planting his hand on the counter, he breathed out against the trap. There was nothing he could say. Her eyes singed through him. He rubbed over his bald head before tugging on his beard.

"What happened?" he asked the floor. "Is it what I think it is?"

She leaned into the counter, abandoning the glass on the granite and swiping her face. She wanted to scrub and scratch the entire night out of her mind. "As far as I can tell. She wouldn't tell me anything. Colin, she is petrified."

He gagged and flinched beside her. "Autumn." He waited until she met his eyes. "We have to report it."

Glaring at him, she pinched the bridge of her nose. "Don't make me explain this to you," she said into her palm. "You know what it's like for women to report a crime. Don't make me explain how much harder it is for women like us."

He opened his mouth, then closed it. Again, there was nothing he could say. There was no argument he could make.

"We have to do something," he finally mumbled back to his feet.

"We *are* going to do something. It's time, Colin. It's time for the plan."

He looked up, features heavy with pain.

"I am going to get Ricky and Willow over here," she continued. "Then, we are going to do something."

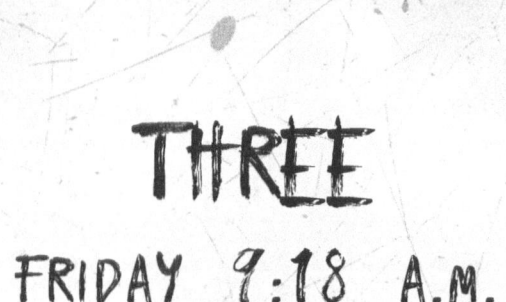

THREE
FRIDAY 9:18 A.M.

STUDENTS STREAMED DOWN the hall past Talia's locker. She watched for an instant, trying to focus on the faces or voices passing by, but the sea of their chatter washed over her like waves. Her consciousness receded, trying to drift from her flesh like a tethered balloon. No matter how bright the hallway was, the image of red and blue lights reflecting on shattered glass flickered over her sight.

Her locker creaked as she opened it. Running her hand over her forehead and hair, she checked her eyes in the mirror. They had the customary hollowness, the detachment. She blinked hard, trying to bring herself back. In the reflection, she caught Willow's strawberry hair behind her, bobbing up above their peers. She appeared from the flow of students, her ample hips guiding her way.

"Hey Tal," she said, grinning wide.

Talia glanced at herself once more before pressing her locker closed. Leaning against it, she crossed her arms loosely over her belly.

Willow knotted her hair on top of her head. Wayward strands wisped around her face to look casual and haphazard, but Talia knew Willow had scrutinized them in her bathroom to get them placed perfect. She had also already seen Willow's Instagram story capturing it.

"Hey Willow," Talia said.

Willow's blue eyes widened as she reclined beside Talia. She shrugged her shoulder into Talia's. Talia knew that gaping look on Willow's face. She was like this every year, every time they hit the anniversary. Her lips drew in on the sides, pursing into a worried little pink flower on her chin. All that rippling feeling made Talia uncomfortable, made her want to shrink away from Willow, but she knew Willow would only follow her.

Willow had been following her for years, since before there was an anniversary.

"How are you doing?" Willow was using her gentle voice. It grated along Talia's nerves, but she kept a soft smile on her lips.

"Fine," Talia said, watching the other students pass by. "History was shit."

"I know, but I mean…" Willow pressed on Talia with those wide eyes.

"I said, fine."

Willow released her pursed lips in a quick grin and dropped her eyes to the tiled hallway.

"*Chicas!*"

Ricky spiraled out of the traffic and slammed into the lockers on the other side of Talia. His dark hair formed perfect spirals on the top of his head. The curls did not even jostle when he hit the metal.

A thin mustache shadowed his upper lip as it curled into a sinister morning smile.

"Where have you been?" Willow glared around Talia at Ricky.

"Latinx Club met this morning before class. Post *Día de los Muertos* for planning next year. I was late to homeroom." Ricky straightened the collar of his shirt, then brushed it flat along his chest.

"But you know what day it is." Willow lowered her voice and tipped her messy bun at Talia.

"I said, I'm fine." Talia rested her head back on the locker, cushioned by her curls.

Ricky snatched Talia in his arms, squeezing her in a quick hug. When he released her again, she could not resist returning his grin. His smile seemed to have extra teeth when he stretched it so far.

"Now, she's fine," he said to Willow. "Well then, what are we doing tonight?" Ricky tipped his chin to give Talia his wide brown eyes, looking to swallow her just like Willow's.

It felt like they both wanted to hold her in their hands so tight they would crush her. Like every year.

"I don't know yet," Talia said. "You know my parents usually want me around today."

"I know," Ricky said. "But that doesn't mean we can't be around too. Remember last year they let us have that pizza movie night?"

Willow and Ricky closed together in front of Talia, pairing their glistening eyes into a probing wall. The warmth of their affection suffocated her. Passing period suddenly stretched into eternity, when they could stare at her until she started to decompose.

"I know." Talia pushed up and away from the lockers. "I'll find out what my parents want to do, and we can figure it out." She offered them both a convincing smile. "Hey, I have to get to chemistry."

"See you in Safe Space at lunch?" Ricky asked.

"Yeah, I'll be there."

Talia nodded to her friends and fled their company, merging into the trickling stream of students. She tried to clear her mind, to think of nothing, to be vacant by the time she found the door to chemistry class.

As Safe Space concluded, the students around them gathered their trash and moved toward the door. Ricky slumped, dramatic, and collapsed on Talia's shoulder. As he groaned into the plume of her hair, Talia reached up to pat his shoulder.

"I'm so tired, *chica*," Ricky grumbled. "Why did they outlaw energy drinks at this school?"

"I'm pretty sure because they are poison," Talia laughed.

"Yes, but I need that kick."

"Maybe you should have eaten more than a salad and some fucking Brazil nuts. Especially with how your mom cooks. Bring some leftovers."

"I'm trying to stay a snack." Ricky pushed up from the desk and gathered his empty dish.

"Oh yes, keep all those football boyfriends happy." Talia smiled at him sideways.

"We are at Safe Space. Do not slut shame me."

"No shame. No shame." Talia tossed up her hands in surrender. "With all your extra classes and clubs, I don't know how you have time for any boys, let alone more than one."

"Bitch, I'm breaking generational cycles." Ricky stood and leaned to the side for theatrical effect. "I'm not ending up wrapped up in some high school loser. I am trying to ride a scholarship far away from here. I'm not trying to get entangled." The smile on his lips drooped. "I'm going to be different. I couldn't stop my dad. I couldn't save my brother. But I won't be them."

"You're already not them. You need to calm down before you kill yourself." Talia stood, gathering her bag.

Ricky slapped at her shoulder. "No one is dying here. Let's go find Lo."

Talia shook her head as she followed Ricky from the classroom. They found Willow against a pillar in the hallway, waiting for them.

"Where were you at, ally?" Ricky spread his arms wide as he approached Willow.

Willow donned a smirk as she stood. "I told you I was having lunch with Jeremy today. Football stuff."

"Ricky has hooked up with every non-straight member of the football team, and you still see him showing up," Talia chimed in.

"Bitch!" Ricky whirled around and hissed. "But some of the straight presenting ones too, though."

The three formed a circle, giggling around the joke. Talia forgot the flickering lights, forgot the broken glass and the cries, forgot the day they meant.

"I believe we were dragging Lo, not me," Ricky said.

"Right, right. We were discussing how our white, straight bestie picked a lunch date over Safe Space," Talia said.

"I miss one time!" Willow exclaimed. "What did you all decide about Trans Awareness Month?"

"We got distracted talking about supporting Homecoming." Ricky rolled his eyes.

Willow shifted her weight to one hip. "This happened last year. Everyone got wrapped up in having queer Homecoming, and we had no budget left for November. We just hung some pink and blue shit in the hall."

"Uh oh, she's a woke white girl." Ricky crossed his arms and leaned toward Talia.

"Oh no, that's the worst kind. Next thing you know, she'll be telling us what all our problems are." Talia crossed her arms the same and leaned against Ricky, speaking as if whispering in his ear.

"Right before she tells us how to fix all our problems." Ricky pointed at the air in front of Willow.

"That she probably caused." Talia tapped her chin.

"That she will probably charge us to fix." Ricky tipped his head against Talia's.

"Just the worst." Talia cheesed her grin at Willow.

"Ugh, you guys!" Willow tossed up her hands, smiling.

"Now, she's misgendering you," Ricky said. "Us, misgendering us. Only *chicas* here, *chica!*"

Willow released an exasperated sigh as Ricky and Talia erupted into laughter. Their giggles eroded the ridges on the day, smoothing it into normalcy.

The tone of the bell shuttered the speakers above their heads. In unison, they raised irritated eyes to the sound. Their chuckles died, and their cheeks slackened.

"So tonight?" Willow's eyes turned into deep blue pools again.

Talia's chest constricted. "Nothing from my mom yet."

"You going to basketball tonight?"

"Yeah, of course." Talia turned to head down the hall.

"Message us after, *chica.*" Ricky raised a hand as the trio dispersed. "I have the hospital, but after that, I'm all yours."

"Bro, you do too much," Willow said.

Ricky pursed his lips.

"You do, though," Talia joined. "You can only take on so much, support so many."

"You know me. I will always be there to support someone who needs it."

Talia knew his compulsion to help was because once, no one helped him. She was not the only one with dark memories and unsavory anniversaries.

Talia looped her thumbs into the straps of her backpack and looked down the empty hall. The rows of lockers seemed to wobble and pulsate the longer she stared. The sounds of people closing lockers, chattering, moving in the hallway dwindled and faded until only her own breathing remained. She could almost hear the seconds ticking from the classroom clocks, one by one.

Somehow, in the breath between each second, she heard her mother screaming—*Juni! Juni!*—before the name dissolved into inhuman shrieks.

"Talia." Her name rolled on the low voice, and a ripple climbed her spine.

Devon stepped around Talia, his sneaker squeaking softly on the hallway tile. He came close, close enough to ruffle the air against her, then settled beside her to trace her stare.

"Don't you have practice, girl?" he asked, his voice still a soft brush on her hearing.

Talia pried her eyes from the doors to the gym and turned them to Devon. He gazed down at her. At contact with his dark eyes, another surge swept up her back.

"Yeah," she said, looking back at the doors.

"You cutting?" He slid his hands into his pockets, elbow turned out enough to nearly press against her.

"Yeah, I think so."

"Cool." Devon licked his lips slowly as a few quiet seconds ticked between them. Then he faced her again. "Can I ask you something?"

"Yeah."

"You and Mia. Is that over?" His eyes rested steadily on her. They did not deepen. They remained solid on the surface.

"Yeah. We broke up a couple weeks ago." Her heartbeat announced itself in her ears.

He nodded softly. "Is it true you're into dudes, too?"

Heat flushed her skin. She skipped a breath as sweat prickled under her arms. She kept her face placid. "Yeah, I'm pan."

"Cool." A smile branched across his cheeks, and he smoothed it down with his hand. "I'm having a party tonight. You want to come?"

The noise of skidding shoes, bouncing balls, and shouts of practice drifted from the gym. The grin brewed in her cheeks as her heart kept whispering in her ear.

She thought of Willow and Ricky with their wide and concerned eyes.

She thought of her parents and all the inevitable tears waiting at home.

"Yeah." She tempered the smirk when she looked at him. "That sounds good."

FOUR
SATURDAY 2:36 A.M.

AUTUMN CALLED RICKY, then Willow, then held her phone in her hand. She gazed at the bright screen until it darkened before lowering it to the counter. Guilt nibbled at the pit of her stomach, somewhere beneath the turmoil and purpose. She turned to find Colin staring at her.

"Autumn." Her name strung tight between his teeth. "What the hell are you doing?"

"Handling this. We're not leaving her alone when we go." She turned her hard eyes to him before walking out of the kitchen.

Emotion roiled beneath her surface. Her child was home, safe and alive, tucked in her bed above them. That should have been enough. But it wasn't. Now, it was time for the rage.

Popping up from the couch, he chased after her. "What are you talking about? We aren't leaving her. We gave up the plan years ago. We put that behind us."

"Who said I did?"

"Autumn, we were never going to really do it. It was our way of—I don't know—dealing. Our way of processing what happened."

Halfway down the hall, she stopped and turned back. She breathed down toward the floor then reached up to gather him by the shoulders. Why didn't he know? Why wasn't he already getting ready? Why hadn't he always been ready for something like this to happen again, like her? Her hands sunk into his flesh, clutched him tighter than she intended. Prying them free, she migrated them to the sides of his face. His eyes wavered, growing waterier as she struggled.

"Someone hurt our baby." She forced the words from her mouth. "She has—" She swallowed. "Bruises and scratches. Her pants are torn. She won't tell me anything."

He stilled at her words. Heat blossomed under her hands.

"We both know what that means," she continued.

His eyes said he knew. His tensed muscles caused him to inflate.

"Okay." His voice deepened, steadied. The color flushed back into his face. "But the plan? The plan was never for this."

"Close enough." Releasing his face, she whirled back toward the garage.

"Autumn." He matched her steps. "We need to calm down and think about this first."

Halting, she spun again. Her mouth turned up, yet her eyes remained heavy, determined. She pressed her lips gently against her husband's, savoring the warmth of his skin, brushing her fingertips along the length of his beard. Then she retreated and offered the same empty grimace.

"Go check on your daughter before her friends get here," she said. "I'll get things together. Don't say anything about us leaving. She's scared enough."

She turned back around, the pineapple fan of her curls spiraling with her before bouncing into place atop her head.

Colin watched the dance of Autumn's hair as she marched into the shadows and into the garage beyond them. He wrapped his fist around his beard and pulled the hair taut, tugged until he felt sharp pains zing along the follicles. Then he shifted back through the house to mount the stairs.

The eyes of their family photos on the hall wall seemed to follow him. The smiles suddenly looked strained. The fractured collage no longer glinted in happy memories. Juni's angelic face appeared ready to yell at him.

He eased up to Talia's door as his heart eased up into his throat. His breathing crowded around the lump. He wanted to burst through the door and gather Talia in his arms, hold her tight, and bring her to a hospital or the police, somewhere that felt safe and like he was doing something. He also wanted to flee back down the stairs and find out what the hell Autumn was packing, what supplies they needed for her plan.

They should be focused on Talia, not some vigilante plan. You called the authorities in these situations. You reported to the police. That was what he had always believed. Until he married Autumn. Until that one night. Now, even as his instincts balked, he couldn't argue with her. He couldn't tell her they could go for help, and it would be all right.

They had the plan for a reason.

He rapped on the door with light knuckles, sucked in a deep breath, and pushed into the room.

"Tal?" he called.

The air in Talia's room was different. A cold current snaked through it, charged with anxious energy. Or maybe that was his emotion rolling ahead of him in waves. Talia had a dim light beside her bed illuminated. Her eyes found her father like smoldering coals, glowing as they tracked him.

"Hey Daddy." Easing up to her elbows, she drew the blankets up to her chin.

"You let your mother braid your hair." A smile mused on his lips, ruffling his mustache.

She flicked her eyes up toward her own scalp. "Yeah. It seemed to relax her."

Lowering himself to the mattress beside his daughter, he extended his hand to place on her knee then retracted it to his own lap. He shouldn't touch her right now. She should come to him.

"What about you? Are you okay?" he asked.

She looked down at her lap. He could see her hands shifting nervously under the covers.

"Maybe that's a stupid question to ask," he said, reaching for his beard again.

"No, Daddy." Her lips curled weakly as she glanced at him. "I'm fine. What did Ma—" She took a deep breath, raising her chest beneath the blanket. "Tell you?"

He finally hazarded the touch and pressed his hand to where he thought hers were. "She told me enough."

Her breath hitched as tears swelled into her eyes, extinguishing the copper coals. "I'm sorry, Daddy," she croaked. "I promise nothing happened. I promise I'm fine." Her fingers emerged to grope at him as her breathing quickened.

The tragic crack in her voice shattered him. The fractures filled in with something hot. "Oh no, baby," he insisted. "It's not your fault." He tried to damper the desperation in his words, but he needed her to know that.

Talia shrugged, dropping her head.

"What can I do, Tal?" he asked, quiet and soft. "How can I help?"

She scooted to a seat. The blanket tumbled from her shoulders to pool in her lap. "No." Her voice quivered on the word. "No help. I told Ma. It was nothing, and I'm fine."

Watching her lie cut him. The slice across his heart burned, then solidified something in him, brought Autumn's preparations back into his mind.

Lifting his arms, he offered Talia his embrace. She dove into him, and the impact was sweet nostalgia on his skeleton. Holding her calmed him, having her tangibly safe in his arms at that moment. He knew exactly where she was. He knew he was between her and the rest of the world. He clung to her and that serenity until the embrace seemed to sedate her as well.

Then the doorbell resonated through the house.

"Ricky and Willow must be here."

Her eyebrows lifted and eyes dilated. Colin could not tell how she was reacting or what she wanted.

"Do you want to come down? Or do you want me to send them up?" he asked.

She raised her face to her father, her eyes fat with threatening tears. His chest clutched at the sight of their menace.

"Send them up." She slid down her pillow.

Grasping the blanket, he moved it up to her shoulders, pressing the fabric along her chest and tucking it against the sides of her arms. Loose like he did when she was young. She never wanted to feel pinned. That echo broke his heart again. Before his own eyes could swell, he bent down and pressed his lips to her warm forehead.

"I will," he said.

Before Talia could question anything, Colin slipped from the room and closed the door behind him. Behind the door, he let the heat bubble inside him. As he descended the stairs, he could hear the jittery voices filling the rooms below.

Autumn stood behind the kitchen island; her palms pressed into the countertop. She had already placed steaming cups before Ricky and Willow. Willow drew a stool and crumpled atop it in her fluffy pajama pants and oversized hoodie. Nothing she would be caught dead posting online. Ricky stood beside her, shifting his weight from side to side before pacing along the edge of his space, dressed as if ready to be out for the day, hair even in place.

"She said you wanted her home." Willow drew her mug close and wrapped both hands around it. "For the anniversary," she said to the quivering surface of the milky coffee.

Autumn leaned forward on her arms and hung her head between her shoulders. "She told us she was with both of you, having a movie night at your house to distract herself." She nodded at Willow.

"Where was she?" Colin asked, moving into the room.

All eyes turned to him. He marched around the island and beside Autumn, extending a hand to rest on the small of her back. She felt the solidarity in it. Willow offered him a weak smile as Ricky stopped pacing long enough to nod.

"What happened to her?" Ricky asked, pinning his arms across his chest.

Colin cradled Autumn's shoulders. They exchanged a glance and a heavy sigh. Autumn pressed her lips together and looked between Ricky and Willow.

"She said she got drunk and fell," Autumn said. "That's not what her injuries say. Someone hurt her." She snagged the words before she described the ligature marks, the bruises, the strange welt that already looked like a scar.

"Fuck!" Ricky hissed as he spun away from the counter. He spiraled back and raised his hands. "*Lo siento.*"

Willow covered her mouth and collapsed onto her elbows. Ricky pulled another stool out and dropped into it, neglecting his black coffee.

"What do you need us to do?" Ricky asked, fists clenched in front of him.

"Be there for Talia," Autumn answered. "Stay with her while Colin and I go take care of something."

Ricky looked down at his fists and nodded slowly.

"Shouldn't Talia go to the police or the hospital or something?" Willow asked.

Autumn and Ricky locked eyes briefly. They both glanced at Willow before ignoring her question, Colin watching them.

"No," Colin said to Willow. "She's safest here." He clutched Autumn a little tighter and caught her eyes. "We're going to handle it."

"What does that mean?" Willow stiffened on her stool.

Ricky snagged Willow by the back of the elbow. He shook his head, near imperceptible, and widened his eyes at her. She read the message and pursed her lips in receipt, rising from her stool.

"We'll be here as long as you need," Ricky said.

"Thank you, Ricky," Autumn said. "Please don't tell her we've gone. We want her to stay calm and rest."

Ricky frowned, then abandoned it, nodding. Willow opened her mouth, but before she could question them, Ricky looped his arm through hers and led her away. They walked across the room like dates headed to a dance, ascending the stairs entwined until even their feet marched up out of sight. Autumn and Colin leaned against the counter, watching them go. Colin offered the back of Autumn's neck a soft squeeze.

Once they were alone downstairs, Autumn marched back to the garage. Colin followed her through the door, closing it softly behind them. She dragged a black bag across the workbench, the sound of metal, canvas, and friction. When she turned to him, he shied from the sight.

"I never thought I would see that again," he said.

"My kill bag." She dropped her focus to the zipper and wound her hands in the straps. The weight of the bag comforted her, the way it always did when she loaded it into the trunk. "I used to drive by his house," she said to the kill bag. "All the time those first years. I had to be prepared." Steel eyes to him. "In case I could ever do it."

She expected his cringe, his retreat, the silent judgment he never breathed life into with words. The plan had always made him uncomfortable, even in his blackest grief. She didn't think he could ever completely let go of the idea that something like that couldn't happen to them. To him. As they plotted, she suspected he was in it more for her than himself. It was his way to calmly let her rage.

Instead, he withdrew his hands and walked to the dented metal cabinet in front of her sedan. Crouching, he spun a combination into the dangling lock and opened the door. She had never seen in the cabinet, never asked, never cared. A man needed a cabinet of privacy in a house of women. Extracting a black case, he returned to her, placing the case beside the bag. He spun the numbers into the lock. She knew them.

Juni's birthday.

He cracked the case open to expose a gun and a corresponding clip nestled in padding.

"Unregistered," he said. "No serial numbers."

Maybe he had been in the plan for himself just as much as she was. Maybe he also had explored tangential revenge fantasies without her. Without a word, she opened the bag to receive the weapon.

FIVE
FRIDAY 8:42 P.M.

THE SHOT SIZZLED down Talia's throat, carving burning lines behind her molars before blooming in her belly. Her throat flexed around the heat as she clamped her teeth down to restrain it.

"There you go," Devon cheered, pushing a Solo cup into her hand.

Talia plastered a smile over the grimace and sipped from the red cup. The sour beer diluted the burn and allowed her to straighten up again. The buzz crept up from her frothing stomach, sweeping a haze from the back of her brain and stretching tingles down her limbs. She felt the edge of the pleasant numbness she was chasing—detachment, a layer of padding between her and this night.

They tucked into the corner of the kitchen counter, slouching beside the fridge. The house teemed around them. Music thumped like a heartbeat under exaggerated chatter and colliding laughter. Kids from school moved and flowed through the rooms in a faceless blur. Just as they did in the hallways. She didn't even bother trying to identify them.

Her eyes fluttered closed for a brief instant as a grin snuck onto her face. When she opened them again, Devon was watching her. She giggled and brought her hand over her mouth.

"What?" she laughed.

"You," he said into his cup as he took a drink.

"D! Yo, D!" A voice called from the crowd. "You gotta get in on this."

Devon peered over at the beer pong game on the table. "Hey, I'll be right back," he said to Talia.

Talia nodded and lifted her cup to Devon as he shuffled through the crowd. He turned sideways to slip through four cheerleaders in tight crop tops and high ponytails, faces lit by their phone screens. He grasped the doorframe as he passed through half the basketball team to take his place behind the triangle of beer cups. Trent, tall, pale, and lanky, extended his arms in a puffed up challenge.

Talia watched Devon square up and pluck a ping-pong ball from the table. Screens glowed as the spectators stood poised to take video clips of the game. He launched the ball toward Trent's triangle. It tapped the edge of the first cup before tumbling into the next. The table erupted in cheers as Trent fished the ball out and drank the contents. Talia eased away from the counter and slunk from the kitchen.

As she rounded into the hallway, she glimpsed Mia loitering along the wall behind the beer pong game. Mia wound her fingers around a section of her sleek, black hair, smoothing the length over and over in a hypnotic rhythm. Talia felt the trance taking over her, felt herself staring at Mia like she used to, but Mia nibbled her bottom lip at Chloe. Her shoulders rocked gently as she talked. The language was too familiar. Talia snapped her attention away and hurried to the couch.

Dropping into a heap on an empty cushion, her inebriated brain bounced in her skull before settling. She cuddled back into the couch, savoring the reverberation on her nerves, feeling everything and nothing. She floated away from the day and the guilt at not being with her parents or Ricky and Willow.

"Oh hey, Talia," Alexis said as she and Morgan claimed the cushions beside her.

Talia sat up on the cushion, smiling at them.

"You skipped practice today." Alexis sang the words as she clamped the rim of her cup between her teeth, still clad with metal braces. The brackets were looped with the school colors of black and gold.

"I did." Talia made a concerted effort to speak crisply and not slur her words.

"Coach was not pleased." Alexis *tsk*ed her finger in front of her cup, still dangling from her teeth.

"Girl, don't listen to her." Morgan leaned onto Alexis's knee, scrolling through her phone screen. "Coach did not even notice. He was too busy torturing us. Suicides, so many suicides." She shook her head and collapsed into Alexis.

"He's not going to miss me." Talia lifted her cup and drained it into her mouth. "I don't even start."

Alexis and Morgan continued to complain about the practice Talia had spared herself. Talia kept her eyes on them, nodding and laughing at the right pauses, yet her mind wandered. She tumbled back into herself, ignoring the darkness to focus on just the float.

"Hey Talia," Devon called, back in the kitchen. "Need a refill?"

Alexis and Morgan both raised their eyebrows above mischievous grins. Talia toasted them with her empty cup then wrangled herself to her feet.

"Did you win?" Talia asked as she pushed back into the kitchen.

Devon reached for her cup. "What are you talking about? Of course, I won. Celebratory shots?" The syllables tangled in his grin.

She nodded, reclining into the counter. Sharp emotions climbed her spine like a ladder, and she salivated to wash them back into darkness. Party music surged, the bass climbing her legs through the soles of her shoes. Waves of laughter and cheers rose in response. The house swelled with sound.

She seized the shot from him, almost too eagerly, then made herself wait, force the smile, cheers before downing it. When the heat spread through her, she kept her eyes closed too long. The clock waited for her when she surfaced, blinking and glaring to remind her it was still November 11th. She did not tame her reaction fast enough.

"Talia?" He leaned in, face painted with the concern she hated.

"Yeah." She brought herself back, recomposed her face. "Fine."

He slid the shot glass from her hand, discarding it and drawing close. He brought his mouth beside her ear, sowing conspiracy under the clamor of their classmates.

"Liar."

The word dripped down her neck, drawing gooseflesh up her arms. The objection formed on her tongue, but the lubricated truth slipped out first.

"I'm not supposed to be here. I'm supposed to be home."

He retreated enough to regard her face, gathering his cup into his chest. "Parents don't like you out?"

Her smirk was bitter, a twitch then release. "Not really. Not tonight."

"What's tonight?"

"An anniversary."

"Of what?"

"Something bad." That was enough. She chomped down on her tongue to disable it. Confession was not a distraction. She brought herself back to her motivation for being here at all and tilted her head. "I thought you were getting me a refill."

His eyes narrowed, and he examined her for a breath. She solidified her surface, seated the *I'm fine* mask into place. When he did not wilt, she raised her eyebrow and ran the tip of her tongue over her smile. That changed his face, melted his curiosity.

Stepping against her, he lowered his lips beside her ear again, close enough to brush against her skin. "How do you feel about going upstairs instead?"

Talia smirked to herself and nodded. His face split into a grin, and his hand slithered into hers. His guidance steadied her as she wobbled after him up the stairs.

SIX
SATURDAY 2:51 A.M.

TALIA BURROWED INTO her mattress, head peeking out from the mound of comforter her father had secured around her shoulders. Ricky leaned against the headboard beside her. Willow curled up by the shape of her feet. They both attempted to relax as they listened to her, but Talia could feel the anxiety radiating off them in itching waves. Worse than their concern, their pity from earlier, their tight exhalations poisoned the air with subdued panic.

Ricky scrutinized her puffy eyes and battered appearance as she confessed her attendance at Devon's party. The shots, the hookup, more shots. The way her mind spiraled away from her in all those terrible anniversary echoes.

Ricky frowned and gave his head a small shake. "But why? We would have gone to the party with you."

"Because I just wanted to get fucked up." Talia returned her eyes to her hands. "And neither of you like when I get fucked up."

Talia felt them cringe. It was the unspoken thing between them. That Talia was drinking and partying too much. That she was sloppy when she did, and it was only making things worse. That they were, once again, worried about her. She didn't need to see their expressions; they were the ones she had been avoiding with her lies. By the time Talia glanced up, they gave her calm faces.

"Did something happen at the party?" Willow asked. "Did Devon or someone hurt you there?"

Ricky grimaced at the question, then moved toward Talia, poised to comfort her, prepared to catch her.

A grin bunched Talia's cheeks. She shook her head. "No. I slept with Devon." She paused and looked between them. "Quite willingly."

At the words, she remembered lazy butterflies circling below the weight of her buzz, causing her to waver in the dim light of his room. When she forgot to think about Mia downstairs or the rumors it would start or if he had the right protection or if she liked him enough to want to hook up more than once. When she disappeared under his body, melting into a blur of breath and sensation, chasing just the feelings on her nerves.

"Oh, shit!" Ricky gasped. "Finally."

"Jeremy said he had just been waiting for you to be over Mia to make his move," Willow added.

They watched her a beat, leaned forward, waited for the reveal.

"So, nothing happened at the party?" Willow asked.

"No, the party was fine." Talia sat up straighter, blowing out a breath. "After Devon, the day just kind of got to me. I took some shots, got real drunk, and just took off."

She had felt the party behind her as she toasted the night and threw the shot back. She could not feel the burn as much that time.

Her intoxication flared, making her eyelids feel heavy and body distant.

She turned unfocused eyes to the microwave clock. Still November 11th. She took another shot.

The party hazed into the distance as the silence in her mind grew deafening. In the crowded house, she felt alone with her hands pressed to the counter. There were tiny bloody hands and shattered glass. She thought of how alcohol had brought her to this moment.

She took yet another shot.

"What?" Willow's voice brought her back.

"Took off? Like, drunk and by yourself?" Ricky's mouth dangled after his words.

Heat bloomed unseen on Talia's cheeks. "I told you, it's all my fault."

Ricky lay his hand on the blanket beside Talia, palm up, uncurling his fingers. Talia glanced down and slipped her hand into his. He and Willow sat in vibrating patience. They chewed on responses, keeping their mouths shut.

"So, I left the party," Talia continued. "I was drunk, and I went to walk home. I think. I just had to get out of there, and my head was a mess. I ended up on Monere."

"Monere? In the dark? Alone? Why the fuck were you on Monere? Those woods are always fucking creepy. Could be high noon. Doesn't matter." Ricky squeezed Talia's hand.

Willow nodded until her messy bun bobbed in agreement.

"Mr. Rudolph went up there to prove that it was all local legend. Never saw him again," Ricky said.

"Mr. Rudolph left his wife and ran off with Kaylee Murphy," Willow sighed.

"But they found all those people up there," Ricky continued.

"Enough." Willow raised her hand. "We all know. Go ahead, Tal."

"For fuck's sake, *chica*!" Ricky threw up his hand. "I cannot handle this suspense!"

"Ricky!" Willow hissed. "I swear if you say *chica* one more time."

"Oh, bitch," he breathed. "Do not come for my crutch word in a time like this."

Willow rolled her eyes. "Take your time, Tal."

"Take your time?" Ricky raised an eyebrow at Willow. "Who are these fucking weirdoes? What did they do to her?"

Willow glowered at Ricky. "This is not being supportive."

"It's fine. It's fine," Talia hushed.

Ricky and Willow glared at each other before returning their eyes to Talia. Talia pressed her teeth into her bottom lip until it trembled under her bite. Tears escaped down her cheeks as she looked up at them.

Then, she took a deep breath and told them.

Autumn curled against her car door, wrapping her arms around her body, clutching her seatbelt. She remained fixed, staring straight ahead, her mind smoldering under her scalp. The memories swelled over her.

"Mommy!" Talia howled. "You're pulling too hard."

Autumn wrapped her hands around Talia's hair, tugging the curls into a high ponytail, wrangling them into a bun. She ignored her daughter's complaints and glanced at the clock hanging on the hallway wall in the brightly lit dance studio.

Talia abandoned her protests and looked down to her lap. She toyed with the hem of her wispy black skirt, then pinched her pink tights between her fingers, gripping and releasing them over and over.

"*Stop, baby,*" Autumn scolded. "*You'll tear them.*" She glanced down at the floor, ensuring Juniper was still sprawled on the tile with her coloring book.

"*They don't match,*" Talia mumbled.

Autumn secured Talia's hair and leaned back to verify its alignment. "What do you mean, baby? They're the dress code. They match your leo just fine."

Talia pulled forward out of her mother's grip and turned up to face her. "Me. They match the other girls. They don't match me."

Autumn sank her teeth into her bottom lip, closing her eyes. Her heart seized tight as she breathed to keep her face still.

"*They are pink, baby.*" The words tasted sour and felt unnatural on Autumn's tongue. "*It's just the dress code. Now, go on. It's time for class.*"

Talia's eyes smoldered as she looked through her mother. Autumn thought it was with disappointment. She reached down to touch the pillow of Juniper's hair as she watched Talia march in with all the other little girls in pink tights.

Outside, the snowflakes began to flutter down in the darkness.

Autumn flinched, knowing where that night went, seeing Talia's bun lilt and sway as she cried as the paramedics examined her face. Autumn yanked herself from the past. She brought herself back to this night, this plan.

There was only one thought: *Hurt them.* Whoever *they* were.

Colin perched in the driver's seat of the silver SUV the same as he had on the couch cushions, waiting for Autumn. He clung to the steering wheel with one hand while the other smoothed over his beard methodically. His wide, pale eyes flitted between the road and Autumn.

"Where are we going?" he asked.

The streetlights passed over the vehicle, illuminating the seats before the car darkened again. Each light washed over Autumn, and the next found her unchanged.

"Monere Lane." Lifting her chin, she swallowed hard.

"What the hell was she doing on Monere?"

"Walking home from a party. She wouldn't tell me much, but she did say it was the people from Red Walls House."

"But she didn't tell you what they did?"

"No," she said through thin lips.

"So, we don't know."

She turned stiffly toward him. "She's been hit in the face. She has bruises on her wrists from being tied or held down. There are scratches on her stomach and a big welt. Her pants were ripped off. Colin, I *know*."

"Maybe it was at the party, and she doesn't want to tell us?"

"Colin," she repeated. "You didn't see her. I *know*. Red Walls House."

"Holy shit," he breathed. He shifted both hands to the top of the wheel and leaned forward. "I've been scared of that house my whole life."

Autumn finally animated, softening to release her arms. She turned toward him. "We all have." Rubbing her face, her pinkies betrayed a slight tremble. "Turns out we were right."

"Do you remember when they found those mutilated homeless people in the woods?"

"Everyone remembers that."

He seized her hand, clutching it too tight. She didn't mind. She clung to the warmth of his skin, wilting toward their entanglement.

"Why tonight?" she croaked. "Of all nights." She pressed their hands to her forehead. "I can't—Not again—Not tonight." The words stumbled around her contained sobs. Then she sucked in a breath and stiffened again.

He squeezed her hand tighter. "We didn't." He turned his eyes away from the road. "She's home. She's safe."

"But they hurt her." She burned her eyes into him.

"And we are handling it. This time, we're handling it."

A smirk snuck onto her lips. "Not if you don't watch the road."

Colin eased back from the wheel and returned a hand to his beard. In the silence, Autumn's mind became deafening. That night long ago, on a road dark like the one rolling under their tires. Talia battered in the bathtub. Her heart sang a song of her maternal failing.

The familiar route was effortless, yet the air thickened in the car as Monere Lane neared. Tension saturated them, a strange mix of rage and apprehension, edged with stale childhood fear.

"I'm not going to pull up to the house," he said.

"No." She shook her head until her curls bobbed. "Park around the woods, and we'll come up from the back. Did you leave your phone?"

"Yeah," he said. "Back at the house."

"Same," she said.

Colin rolled the car to a stop and killed the engine. Even after he extinguished the headlights, he remained in his same driving position. As if holding still would spare him the moment.

"Are we sure about this, Autumn?" He continued to stare through the windshield. "We should have—" He stopped, swallowing the sentence.

She gripped his shoulder until he looked at her. "We are taking care of our daughter. We can do something this time."

Pursing his lips, he eased from his door, shoes crunching on the road. She did the same and moved to the back of the SUV. Opening the back hatch, she tugged the kill bag toward the bumper. He moved beside her to peer over her shoulder.

"Everything still in the bag?" he asked.

Thinking about the bag stirred something in her. She wasn't sure if it was pride or shame or the stab of painful memories. Touching the straps put her back in a dark driver's seat every night she had not stopped, not killed the drunk man who took Juni from them.

Unzipping the duffle, she exposed the neglected kit. The neatly folded plastic sheeting. The box of latex gloves, the leather gloves. The rolled sleeve of blades. The hammers and screwdrivers lifted from Colin's tools. Not that he would have noticed; he hadn't built or fixed a thing since that night. It would have been fitting to give them new purpose on the ones who did this to Talia.

Maybe they could find the proper sheath tonight.

"What?" she said, a hammer handle in her grasp.

"How do we do this and not end up in prison? At the end of this, we still need to be with Talia." He looked down at the gun.

Releasing the hammer, she sighed. Rage flickered in her eyes. "We follow the plan."

He cast his eyes into the woods.

"We don't have time for this," she said. "They took her. They took our child, and they hurt her. We could have lost another daughter tonight. That piece of shit is still out walking around. Not this time. Not them."

"I know." He placed the gun down beside the bag and pulled her to him, rubbing her shoulders.

Looming over the bag, she held Colin's gun out to him. He retrieved it with a slow, contemplative look at the weapon. She reached for her own, the one they both had known about, small that fit snug in her palm. Something she could conceal. She snatched a pair of leather gloves and offered them to Colin, taking another pair for herself. She slipped folded knives into her pockets, offered Colin brass knuckles. Then she stomped to the trees and waited.

He armed himself in silence. Then he closed the hatch and locked the car, the beeping deafening in the night. She softened as he approached her. They both turned to the woods to glimpse the faint illumination of lights at the top of the hill.

SEVEN
FRIDAY 10:37 P.M.

THE COLD WIND snuck a sharp tongue through Talia's coat to lick along her skin. The chill tickled the distant edge of her intoxication. She stumbled over dead leaves and dragged her sneakers on the pavement. She meandered in the gutter, forsaking the sidewalk to bathe in the dim streetlights.

Her head lolled on her shoulders as she trudged, her eyesight wavering in and out of focus. The identical houses on Devon's street blurred beside her. Yet the texture of the asphalt under her feet remained clear enough. She stared down at it.

A warm tear tumbled from her eye before turning frigid on her cheek. The sliding sensation on her face brought her back to the night. Her feet halted, and she looked around, dazed. She had stumbled far from Devon's street and rounded onto Monere Lane. The shadowed expanse of the woods crawled up the hill beside her.

Surfacing sobriety brought her up into her skin. The alcohol faded so fast. The night chill permeated her coat and then her flesh, reaching its fingers through to her bones. She wrapped her arms tight around herself. Suddenly, the night seemed to close around her, full of sounds.

She hated Monere Lane, as every local child did. The street you walked down faster, even during daylight, and never alone. Yet here she was, planting slanted steps on its pavement, alone in the dark. The street for joy rides after too many drinks for courage. The woods where they had found all those mutilated bodies. Yet here she was, intoxicated and unprotected.

She felt saturated by her stupidity, more drunk on that than the alcohol raging in her veins. She was too far down to turn around. It would be faster to hurry down the hill to the next intersection.

The woods teemed and writhed beside her in breezes and shuffling and a million other distant, unidentified noises. Her mind reeled to form the shapes of the sounds, to shrink them down to things less ominous. Yet her surging heartbeat was not convinced.

Branches snapped nearby in the shadowed forest. Whipping her head toward the noise, she kept shuffling forward, clinging to her sides as she stared into the dark long enough for it to swirl into figments.

Fixating on that swaying black, she hustled down the street. She released her hands, feeling an energy surge sloppily down her inebriated nerves, preparing to run. As she spun around to launch forward, her toe tangled against the asphalt and the weight of her intoxication. Before a thought could flicker across her mind, she careened to the ground.

Her head bounced off the cold pavement. Her drunken hands failed to shield her, instead scraping along the street as she fell. The forest seemed to silence with the sound of her fall and the air whooshing out of her lungs. She coughed and sputtered with the shock, in the hanging moment before her nerves started reporting the damage.

As she lay immobile on the asphalt, the steam from her breath curled back in her face from the ground. Her body hummed as the pain points began to light. Her eyes filled with rushing tears that splattered to the pavement.

"I'm so fucking stupid," she said to the ground, sobs creeping into her throat. "What am I doing? What the fuck am I doing?"

Talia rolled onto her back with no thought of the dirt and leaves weaving their way into her curls. She ignored the burn from her skinned palms and knees, and the radiating aches beneath. She released a deep exhale and watched her own breath swirl between her and the frozen stars.

Her mother would lose her mind if she found Talia splayed out in the middle of a nighttime road. Her parents would be livid if they knew how drunk she was on this night of all nights, if they had any idea how drunk she had been getting recently. They probably could have forgiven any other substance more than alcohol. They would both be so worried if they knew she was out wandering alone, not with Ricky and Willow.

They were all always so worried.

"What am I doing?" she whispered as she dragged herself from the ground.

Her pain folded beneath the wave of her guilt and regret as she stood, pouring down inside her like hot tea down her throat. She glared down the hill with singular purpose. She needed to undo this. She needed to get home.

"What are you doing, little lamb?" The voice came from behind her, as if it materialized out of the night itself.

Fear sliced through Talia's heavy sadness, bringing her back to the vivid moment. Swallowing the gasp, she flinched and turned. Two tall, pale figures loomed on the road, as if they had always been standing over her crumpled body.

The woman's flaxen hair snaked in three braids down her scalp before releasing and cascading into waves past her shoulders. It floated and swayed in the soft moonlight. Her icy eyes gleamed as she stared into Talia. Talia recoiled from the menacing sight of her. The woman towered above her in a long, black lace dress that clung to the wide curves of her body.

The man beside the woman planted his feet and dug massive fists into his hips. His scalp shined completely bald, and a wiry blonde goatee sprouted from his chin, the hair dangling toward the center of his inflated chest. He stood shorter than his companion, yet still eclipsed the moon above Talia. His eyes were narrow yet just as icy as the woman's.

Talia shrank back, her arms back around her waist, as if she could protect herself. She scrutinized the pair, prickling with panic, completely unsure what to do. Her heart pounded hard enough that it throbbed on the sides of her vision, rippling the edges of the night around the two pale figures.

"I said." The woman took a step forward. "What are you doing, little lamb?" She glowed in the moonlight, her hair, her skin shining in the dim light. Her height seemed monstrous as she grinned down at Talia and extended her hand toward her face.

"Lina," the man hissed from behind her. "Are you sure?"

"Hush, Lamont." Lina cast a glance back over her shoulder at him before sending her piercing stare back through Talia.

Talia scrabbled back and to her feet, but she remained rooted to the asphalt. Her sneakers felt akin to the trees in the spooky woods beside them. She became her heartbeat, still thundering through her veins.

"Walking," Talia answered, forcing her shoulders to shrug. She wrenched her gaze from Lina's and willed her feet to scrape along the pavement.

Staggering in awkward steps down the hill, she gave her back to the strangers. She could still feel their cold blue eyes on her. Could sense them moving behind her, though she did not hear the footfalls with hers.

I have to get home to them. Her voice surfaced in her mind, her buzz dissolving beneath her sizzling nerves. *Not tonight. Not tonight. Not tonight. I have to get home to them,* she told herself again.

Lina eased up on the road beside her, swaying in her strides. Her lace dress and fair hair billowed with her movements. Talia halted, and Lina mirrored, turning to face her.

"What are you doing?" Talia squinted.

"Walking." Lina offered Talia's same weak shrug.

Sucking in a breath, Talia nearly choked on the lump swelling in her throat. She whirled back to the road and lengthened her strides. Without effort, Lina matched them.

"Where are you going, little lamb?" Lamont's gruff voice crawled up Talia's back.

She flinched against it. "I'm not a little lamb."

"You look like a little lamb." A sharp grin carved up the side of Lina's face, angling toward her severe cheekbone. "How old are you?"

"Twenty," Talia lied on impulse.

"You smell like a lot of vodka for twenty," Lamont commented.

Talia ignored him and quickened her pace.

"Don't be such a square, Lamont." Lina revealed another vicious grin. "You were drinking long before twenty-one."

"I was doing many things long before twenty-one. Different times." Laughter ruffled the edge of his words.

Talia forced her breath out of her nose as fear constricted her chest. Anxiety flailed through her limbs. The impulse to run flashed repeatedly through her muscles.

What is wrong with me?

What the fuck have I done?

Why did I do this to them?

Why tonight?

I have to get home to them.

I HAVE TO GET HOME TO THEM.

Her thoughts nearly overshadowed the slamming of her heart.

"Are you hurrying home to your parents, little lamb?" Lina glided over her steps as if barely moving.

YES! Please God, hopefully yes. "No." Talia dismissed the question with another shrug.

"Boyfriend?" Lamont asked.

Wrapping her arms around her stomach, she shook her head.

"Girlfriend?" Lamont's voice climbed playfully.

Talia exhaled hard and shook her head harder.

Lina extended her long leg across Talia's path and moved in front of her. Talia nearly collided with her before grinding to a stop on the asphalt.

"So, you are all alone?" Lina bore her eyes into Talia's.

Talia stared back into the frosty blue, thinking about lying to her parents, saying she was with her friends, and about lying to friends, saying she was with her parents and about slipping out of Devon's party the minute he wasn't looking.

Alone. Yes, she was all alone. She felt the depth of the solitude she had crafted.

She didn't even have to answer. Lina's smile crawled up her cheeks.

"Yes, Lamont," she said. "I am sure."

The predatory flare in Lina's grin silenced Talia's relentless heart. Her nerves seized that terrible second before adrenaline surged through her, like the itching anticipation of crouching down with her fingertips on the gym floor before the coach blew his whistle. The cry of sneaker soles skidded on each suicide turn as she clawed to be faster. Her body vibrated in the suspense of that moment.

Lamont ambled around Talia, placing himself beside Lina. Again, he set his feet wide and seated his fists against his hips. At any other moment, Talia might have found his posture comical. She might have waited for him to begin a slow rotation in place, like a video game avatar. Lina stepped toward him and folded her hands on his shoulder, jutting her hip out towards Talia, mocking and casual.

Talia flicked her gaze between the two, their eyes like the blue flame wavering under her water heater that used to scare Juni.

Then she ran.

She leaned into a wobbly sprint down the hill, but Lina swiftly appeared in the road ahead, lace dress ruffling. Skidding to a graceless halt, Talia whirled to climb the street back toward Devon's. Lamont barred her passage. Her mind reeled. After a stuttering dance, she plunged into the woods. From the look of Lina and Lamont, there was a decent chance either one of them could run her down. She had never been the first done with suicides at practice, and most of the opposing point guards outran her. Maybe in the trees she could use her agility. Perhaps in the woods she could find a dark corner to hide in.

Crunching dead leaves and snapping sticks announced Talia's every step as she leaped and barreled through the trees. She careened through the forest in a frenzy, losing orientation in the blur. Plowing over fallen trees and slapping trunks with her scraped palms, she rushed up the crest of the first hill. With the road out of sight, she crouched down and hunkered against a trunk, panting loud, glaring between the stripes of moonlight. When she held still, she could feel her pulse in her blooming bruises.

"Oh, little lamb!" The call drifted on the night.

Talia pressed harder into the tree until she could feel the bark biting into her back. She scanned the night, yet could only make out the stagnant trees.

"Why didn't you say you wanted to play Hide and Seek?" Lina's voice came from the opposite direction and descended into giggles. The laughter wove through the branches, swirling around Talia.

Talia eased away from the trunk and poised to run again.

"What are you doing, little lamb?" Lina boomed from beside her.

Talia snatched her hand over her mouth to smother the scream. Lina looked down at her, amused, before releasing another laugh. Her cackle filled the forest, enlivened the trees. Talia scrambled to her feet and stumbled backward, bloody palms outstretched to receive the incoming trees. Then she whirled and ran deeper into the forest.

The trunks blurred in Talia's vision as she thrashed through them. She tripped and fumbled over rocks, her pace marred by the flailing attempts to keep her balance. Her breath ripped in and out of her lungs until her throat was raw and her mouth dry. Every time the thought *I have to get home to them* flitted through her mind, fresh tears welled in her eyes.

How could I do this to them?

The new thought solidified her muscles. She flinched against the burning in her sinuses, stopping so she could squeeze her eyes shut. When she opened them, she looked at the moon, distant and safe in the sky above her.

How could I do this to them?

Talia released her head, her chin thumping to her chest. When the ground came into focus, she glimpsed a large fallen tree. Squinting, she moved closer. The massive center appeared rotted and hollowed out. Without a thought, she dove in.

The edge of the bark cracked and flaked against her, biting at her skin like so many brittle teeth. Yet the innards of the tree sloughed and caved against her weight, soft as flesh.

Encased in the tree, her own breathing surrounded her. Its panic reverberated through the wood. She concentrated on it until she could slow its pace and volume. Wrapping her arms tight around her stomach, she resolved she could stay tucked within this bark. Until she could go home to them.

A few moments passed, slow and excruciating. She tried to ignore the crawling agitation on her skin. It felt like wriggling insects, or it was wriggling insects. She wanted to scream either way, so she just measured her breathing. Then heavy footsteps approached. They moved in a steady rhythm, pulverizing the leaves and twigs beneath them. They grew closer and closer until they hesitated right outside her tree.

She stopped breathing, buttoned her lips, until her lungs threatened to burst. Holding a quivering hand over her mouth and nose, she stifled her instinct. Then the crawling moved just along her neck. Tiny, scratching legs dragging along her skin. She bottled the cry in her throat, vibrating with restraint, allowing whatever it was to scurry towards her hair.

The footsteps shifted to circle her fallen tree. Once. Twice. Her head swam, heart knocking at her lungs and hand trembling violently at her mouth, before the footsteps finally marched off into the distance.

Releasing her breath in a whoosh, she coughed into her sobs, her heart trying to tear itself out of her inhospitable chest. Shaking, she pushed herself out of the tree, slapping and swiping her neck and through her hair. Even though they were gone, she felt the tiny legs all over her.

With tear tracks frosting her cheeks, she jogged briskly through the trees, aiming for the opposite direction she thought the footsteps had gone. With their heft, they had to be Lamont's. She kept a more moderate pace to avoid tripping and to look back as she moved. She scanned the dark woods over and over, but she could only distinguish the twisted branches of naked trees.

The forest fell silent again around her, reduced to her crunching footsteps and her ragged breathing. The longer she only heard herself, the calmer she became. The more she only saw the dark shapes of trees and rocks, the slower she dropped her pace. At the edge of her mind, she wondered if she had lost them. At the very pit of her stomach, she started to believe she would make it home.

She eased down a hill, walking gently and placing her hand on the trunks as she moved between them. The road glowed below her, like a flat golden snake winding along the edge of the woods. She released a sigh of relief at knowing where she was, at somehow circling back to where she stared.

I'm not going to be this stupid again, she told herself as she approached Monere Lane. *When I get home, I am going to get my shit together. No more of this partying shit. No more of this drinking shit. Definitely no more lying.*

She rattled off her intentions as her sneakers hit the asphalt. She almost smiled until she glanced up the road. Lina, perched on the curb, her long legs extended out in front of her. She had flipped the black lace skirt aside so her pale skin could ignite in the moonlight. Lamont squatted beside her, whittling at a wooden stick with a large, gleaming knife. They both stared at her with their burning blue eyes.

Talia's thoughts evaporated. Her mind turned to static. She stood immobile on the pavement.

Lina's head fell to her shoulder. "What are you doing, little lamb?" She smiled fiendishly.

Talia skidded one foot behind her, then the next, sliding backward gradually.

Lamont rose to his feet and slid the knife into a sheath on his belt. "Enough of this."

Lina rolled her face up at him, the grin still teasing her lips, yet remained where she sat. Lamont rounded her feet and marched toward Talia. He balled his fists at his side and leaned into his approach. Talia's fear returned in a wave. She coiled, turning to flee.

"Don't fight," Lamont commanded. "It will hurt so much more if you fight."

EIGHT
SATURDAY 3:15 A.M.

"Autumn!" Colin said through the trees as he chased her up the shrouded hillside. "Slow down. Autumn!"

Autumn plowed through the woods, directly toward the small squares of light above them. She pivoted and twisted her path around the tree trunks and contours of the hill, almost accelerating at each obstacle. Colin chased her with brisk steps yet lagged farther and farther behind.

"Autumn!" He hesitated against a tree, leaning into the bark with his breath pluming into the night.

She heard him and halted. Pressing her palm into the nearest trunk, she tipped her head to the sky, eyes pinched shut, before she whirled back to him. Her copper eyes singed him even through the night.

"*What.*" She spat the word dead at his feet, no question in it. She was focused. She could see her purpose in front of her. His slow pace, his questions, and the hesitation in them made her nerves bristle.

"We have to run through it again." He stared back at her.

"Run through what?"

"The plan."

She glowered at him, attempting to burn through him, melt him into complacency. He held fast against the tree trunk, moving only with his steady breathing.

"We have had this plan for years." She spoke firm, but her eyes drifted from his face. "We didn't do it last time. This time, I plan to fucking kill them."

"Autumn." He used a gentle, familiar tone and eased up to her. "And then?"

"Then we wrap the bodies in plastic, bring them to the cabin, dismember them, and bury them at the back of the property with lime. We burn our clothes, everything from tonight in the firepit, bury the ashes."

His head bobbed with each recited step. He climbed up to her as their plan dissipated into the night air.

Moving her palm from the tree, she planted her hand over her mouth. She looked back and forth across the night, through the trees. Anything but meeting his eyes. Colin brushed his hand along her face, then cradled her cheek. His warmth radiated into her skin. She wilted against his touch and fought the quiver it inspired in her bottom lip. For a breath, she wanted to fall apart in his arms. Bringing his other hand to her jaw, he drew her toward his chest.

"No, no, no," she murmured into his shirt.

Rubbing his hands along her shoulders, he held her tighter against him. He rested his chin on the pillow of her hair, breathing out into the rigid curls.

Taking a deep breath, she seemed to melt. Then she suddenly planted her fists on his chest and shoved him back. "No, Colin! What is wrong with you? Why are you fighting me on this?"

"I am not fighting you on this."

"They attacked our fucking daughter."

"I'm here with you, aren't I? Following some plan I thought we put to rest years ago." He threw up his hands.

Her eyebrows arched slow. Hip jutted out, her hand found a home perched on it. She held her pose, locked on him.

"Go home if this scares you. Just leave me the car. You can walk from here."

His fingers flexed into fists before immediately releasing. "How could you, Autumn?" His voice dipped low, nearly below the sound of the forest.

"You're the one fighting me on this. You clearly don't want to do this. You want to sit at home while it happens again."

"They're my daughters too, goddammit!" His voice shook the surrounding darkness.

A strange blend of anger, grief, and remorse twisted Autumn's face. Yet she maintained eye contact with him. She resisted the urge to crumple in an apology, to cling to him and release the wave of tears lapping at the edge of her nose.

He stepped up until she had to tip her head back to look at him. "I will not leave Talia all alone."

A tremble crept through her as she looked away. She could not stand Colin threatening her resolve, slowing her down.

"Talia will know what we're doing. Ricky and Willow won't keep her distracted forever," he said.

"But by then, we'll be done. She'll be safe while we clean up."

He caressed her cheek again. "We stick to the plan. We stick together."

The corner of her mouth twitched. "We have a plan, then. Can we go now?"

Colin drew Autumn into his body and clutched her. He put his lips to her temple, leaving a warm trail on her face. She withdrew, brushing her lips along his before spinning from his grasp and back up the hill.

The house grew, sharp and steep, as they approached it until it loomed over them. It sat on the top of the hill, an anticipant giant, porch wrapping around it like a belt. It was dark enough to be its own shadow, save for the glowing rectangles of its windows. The bulbous face of the moon slid behind the wide, steep silhouette of the structure, shrouding them. The night amplified in that extra darkness, feeling safe in concealment yet ominous in possibility.

Autumn went rigid this close to the house. Her nerves rattled, teasing at consummating her goal. Her rage pointed her to a singular focus, as if she was glaring down a tunnel that terminated in a minute point. All she saw, all she felt, was hurting those who'd hurt Talia. She didn't even perceive the night around her or the leaves crunching under her shoes.

Draped in the dark from the house, she moved around the front, past the long porch, and approached the wall, close enough to touch it. The first large window hung dormant, the black shiny surface like a frozen lake at night. She squinted through the pane yet only glimpsed the ghost of her reflection moving over the glass. She slid across it with Colin haunting her steps and eased to the next.

Light spilled from the window, pooling on the fallen leaves and sticks and reaching toward the trunks of the forest, breaking through like a violation in the night. She approached cautiously and avoided it as if exposure could burn her. Yet she craned to see over the sill.

"I see them." Her voice crawled from her mouth so low it was foreign. A tremor seized her calves and crept up her legs until her entire body roiled in a steady quiver.

Colin reached forward and cupped her shaking biceps. He held her in silence until she stilled. Together, they pressed their noses to the edge of the window, creating small halos of fog on the glass.

She settled on the woman first, who extended in a lavish sprawl along the crimson couch. A fire blazed in the massive hearth behind her, casting dancing light over her body. She reclined onto her mane of blonde hair, and the locks flowed over the armrest. Her black lace skirt bunched up above her bent knees to expose pale legs. Thick and defined muscles rippled below her skin as she wriggled her toes. A lazy and contented smile danced upon her lips, and she swirled her hands in the firelight above her.

Across the massive wooden coffee table, littered with a decanter and glasses of liquor, Autumn spotted the male figure she had expected to see. He consumed an indigo armchair, facing the woman. He spread his hefty knees wide and set his elbows on them, bringing his hands together to toy with his large knife. The blade spun between his fingers and glinted in the firelight.

Autumn stilled at the sight. This was not what she expected to see. This was not the intoxicated bunch of young men she thought they would find. This was not who she imagined putting those marks on her child.

"This is who lives in Red Walls House?" Colin breathed into Autumn's hair.

"They're not what I pictured from the stories."

"They look like they're out of an old movie."

Their voices rose, and they hushed themselves, turning back to the glass. The woman's chin wagged and hands gesticulated as she spoke with excitement, though her words did not penetrate the seal on the window. Autumn and Colin could only measure the tones and volume of her speech. The woman's icy eyes sparkled as they moved between the man and the ceiling.

The man responded in low tones, his voice a grumble against the glass. He continued to play with the knife in his hands, yet a smirk lifted the whiskers lining his lip. His cold eyes likewise held an uncanny glimmer.

He discarded his blade to the coffee table and gathered up his glass. The cup disappeared in his massive paw. The woman, taking the hint, drew herself onto an elbow and reached for her own drink. He extended his hand to her, and dipping her chin, she slipped her fingers into his. He pressed his lips to her knuckles. Then they clinked their glasses together and tossed back the liquor.

She threw her head back in laughter as he tugged her up from the couch. His arm moved around her waist as he drew her close to him. They swayed together as they walked.

"They're celebrating," Autumn's voice struggled over her disbelief.

"Are they dancing?" Colin leaned into Autumn to squint through the glass.

"They are celebrating what they did."

What they did to Talia.

Autumn surged toward the window, but Colin clung to her shoulders, hushing into her ear. The sight of the two toasting, dancing, laughing, poured gasoline on the fire in her stomach.

Autumn and Colin remained frozen in the darkness, her insides writhing and smoldering. They watched the pair shuffle and dance away from the couch, across the room, growing smaller as they moved farther from the window. Then their pale swaying shapes were swallowed by the house.

"We go in now," Autumn said.

Colin applied a gentle squeeze to her shoulders again. "Not yet. They may have just gone to get another bottle or some food."

Autumn stamped her foot in an involuntary pout. Her arms drew tight around her body. Yet she waited. She stared at the fire until the flames dissolved into a blur, and she waited.

The moments dragged on, heaping hot and heavy seconds upon them. She shifted uncomfortably under their weight. Her leg shook with increasing fervor as the seconds compiled. She finally turned roasting eyes to Colin. He offered a small nod, the trailing ends of his beard scratching against his coat.

Snaking her fingers into her back pocket, she retrieved the screwdriver and pointed it toward the window.

"Red Walls?" Ricky's voice hushed on the name.

"Oh God." Willow brought her fingertips to her lips. "You've been inside Red Walls House?"

Talia looked down and nodded. Tears sizzled on the back of her sinuses, and she strove to blink them back. She could smell the inside of Red Walls House, feel the cold stone under her back, see the dim red light. Her heart clenched into an angry fist as she tried to focus on her own room around her. Ricky and Willow stared at her, waiting, the air vibrating with tension around them.

"Why didn't you tell your parents?" Willow asked. "Your mom said you wouldn't tell her what happened?"

"She hasn't told us what happened," Ricky murmured.

"It doesn't matter what happened." Talia swiped an errant tear from her cheek. "I knew what they would do. They always had this plan after Juni. My mom said she would never let that happen again. I couldn't tell her because I knew they would go to Red Walls House."

Ricky and Willow exchanged a stretched grimace.

"They didn't," Talia said.

Their faces answered her.

"Fuck!" Talia recoiled. "She promised me! My parents can't be there."

"Your parents will be fine." Willow reached forward to snag one of Talia's hands. She moved her fingers in soothing patterns over Talia's skin.

"Your mom was pre-pared." Ricky fractured the word for emphasis.

"No, you don't understand." Talia withdrew her hand from Willow.

"*Chica*, you should just be glad your parents are willing to throw down for you like this." Ricky reached toward Talia's shoulder.

Talia shrugged him away. "No, it's not about that." Kicking off the blankets, she windmilled her legs from the bed, springing to her feet and pacing along the carpet. "I'm so fucking stupid. How could I do this to them?"

"Talia, this is not your fault." Willow pivoted on the mattress.

"Absolutely not!" Ricky agreed. "You know that from that victims' advocacy event I—"

"Tonight!" Talia threw up her arms, then let them flop to her sides. "The fucking anniversary. What is wrong with me? I almost died, and now I'm going to lose the rest of my family."

"You're not making any sense," Ricky said. He eased along the bed to join Willow at its edge.

"Sit down with us." Willow reached for her. "Tell us what happened."

"I can't be alone." Talia ignored Willow and spoke more to the floor ahead of her. "I can't bury all three of them. This is my fault. This is all *my* fault.

"Talia!" Ricky snapped.

Talia jerked her head, turning to Ricky, then Willow.

"You're spiraling, *chica*." Ricky's tone softened.

Talia halted, exhaling hard. She tried to force the flashes of the night and the smells of Red Walls House from her mind. She tried not to picture her parents on those ragged floorboards. She envisioned them slinking up that staircase toward the room with the red light.

"Your parents are handling it. I'm sure they got this," Ricky said, though his voice lacked its normal punch.

Willow slanted her eyes at Ricky, tipping her chin to him. Talia knelt beside the bed. Balling up her fists on the comforter, she dropped her head to the mattress.

Talia bit at her lip and clutched her own body. "My parents don't know what they're dealing with. These are not normal people."

"Of course, they're not normal," Ricky said. "They kidnapped you and hurt you."

"They're going to kill my parents." Talia's voice wavered as her eyes filled with tears.

"No, they're not." Willow squeezed her knee tighter.

"You're not hearing me," Talia nearly whispered.

Ricky muttered inaudibly in Spanish until Willow glared at him. "Tal, we're here for you. There's nothing you can't tell us," she said. She waited until Talia met her stare. "So, tell us."

"They're not human," Talia squeaked.

"What the hell do you mean, they're not human?" Ricky's voice climbed.

"Like they're monsters for what they did to you? What did they do?" Willow pressed.

"No." Talia's voice rippled in irritation. She rubbed at her face. "No, they are actual monsters. They are not humans."

NINE
FRIDAY 11:11 P.M.

Talia did fight, and it did hurt.

Slung over Lamont's shoulder, a burning ache circled her wrists from where he had seized and wrangled her. Her cheek stung from her squelched opposition. Her body dangled heavily, hands swaying helpless down his back. Hot tears blazed from her eyes and tumbled down toward her fingertips.

She was not going to make it home tonight.

I'm never going to see my parents again, she thought between her stifled cries. *I'm so fucking stupid, and now I'm never going home. They will never recover from this. And I did this to them. On this night.*

She gagged on a sob, and Lamont heaved her higher onto his shoulder.

Oh God, what are they going to do to me?

The last thought silenced her mind, seized it in fear. She did not want to think about it. She would know soon enough.

As Lina and Lamont sauntered through the trees now, Talia could feel Red Walls House looming, the way she could always sense its presence when they drove by or when she and Willow would dare each other to ride up the driveway on their bikes. The house exuded its own force, and Talia felt that menace as they approached it.

Her fear morphed into paralysis. Her emotions vibrated at such a frequency to blur into tranquility. Maybe this is what her therapist would call depersonalization. Maybe this was a situation where depersonalization would finally be beneficial.

She didn't know what to do. A part of her wanted to keep fighting in futility, yet another part wanted to resign to the fate she had purchased with her own carelessness. She had found her way here by wandering to the bottom of a bottle, as if alcohol had not destroyed her family enough. How could she not have learned that already?

Maybe this is what I deserve. Maybe my parents are better off without my bullshit. The thought soured as soon as it lapped upon her brain, yet the depression it conjured lingered, making her heavy. Her body ached for her parents on a primal and cellular level. She wanted her mother to stroke her smooth fingers along her face. She wanted her father to hold her against his broad chest. *Why didn't I just stay home with them?*

She did not dare allow Willow or Ricky or even Devon to flash in her mind, lest it unravel completely.

"I can hear your stomach growling," Lamont said.

His low voice tickled the night. It rumbled against Talia's belly as it shook his shoulder.

"I *am* famished," Lina sang. Her skirt swished through the air as she smashed leaves beneath her.

Boards creaked and whined as Lina and Lamont mounted the sagging porch of Red Walls House. The wood crawled behind

Lamont's heels, and adrenaline surged back down Talia's limbs in a renewed wave. She did *not* want to go into Red Walls House. She couldn't breach that threshold. Arching her back against the idea, she thrashed her legs in Lamont's grip, beat her fists on his back.

Lamont's hands remained fixed and unaffected by her struggles. He marched forward, steady and purposeful. Lina swayed ahead and turned the ornate doorknob. It screeched from the latch, causing Talia's body to go rigid.

"These old and weak muscles," Lina said with a laugh.

"Not for long." Lamont's hand flexed against Talia's leg.

Lina swept through the door and held the large wooden slab ajar for Lamont. As he crossed the threshold, Talia thrust her arms out and clamped desperate hands on the doorframe. Lamont's stride stuttered before he stripped her from the door in one fluid yank. She released a mewling yelp. Her own sound amplified her alarm.

He kicked the door shut behind them, the slam resonating through the large and hollow house.

"Almost time to feast." He sloughed Talia from his shoulder, spilling her onto the dusty hardwood floor.

She collapsed hard onto the boards. The impact echoed up through her knees and elbows, yet she scarcely registered the pain. She scanned the room. A thick coiled banister spilled down the stairs in front of her. Rough walls and dark, smoothed floorboards traced the hallway beside it. Large rooms spread swallowed in shadow on either side of the stairs, one with a massive dining set and the other with a clock calling out each damned second.

It was all a blur as her pulse throbbed in her sight. Curling into a ball, she scrabbled back before colliding with the sealed door.

Lina flicked cold eyes down at Talia, crumpled and cowering against the door. "Revitalization is long overdue."

Lina turned away from Talia to a large mirror hanging in the hallway. She regarded her reflection, bringing her fingertips to her face. Pressing gently, she pushed the flesh back and up in different patterns, chasing a youthful configuration. Then her cold eyes found Talia in the mirror, and the corner of her lips jumped.

"She's perfect," she said to Lamont, though her gaze continued to burn into Talia.

Talia fought to shrink into the door, to press into the wood until she dissolved out of this moment. Against the closed door, at the feet of two giant strangers, she did not know what to do next. Her heart continued to throb, panicked breaths shredded her lungs, yet her brain seemed to abandon her there. Thoughts had evaporated from her mind.

"So young." Lamont's eyes settled on Talia for an instant.

"Young is what I need." Lina's voice curled in a predatory growl, making Talia's blood run cold.

Swirling away from the mirror, Lina planted heavy steps deeper inside the house. Lamont pivoted toward Talia.

"No no no no no," Talia breathed like a mantra.

Lamont's boot landed beside Talia's leg, and fear sent a spire through her chest. At the violent discomfort, she shot to her feet and shoved against the door. She plummeted into the house, sloppy and directionless. She felt the reckless hope running could offer.

Her shoes slapped the hardwood of the huge entry as she clawed the air, trying to swim through the house. The frenzied adrenaline in her chest surged, throbbed in her ears, pulsed through her arms. Her mind collapsed down to a desperate focus.

Get out get out get out get out. Get home to them.

The thoughts pounded in her brain, thick enough to crowd out her other senses.

Lina marched up the thick stairs, trailing her hand along the rough wood of the walls. Her fingertips snagged and bumped along splintered edges, yet she continued to drag her hand unfazed. At the sound of Talia's sloppy sprint, she hesitated in the red glow from an open door at the summit.

Talia did not hear Lamont's thick boots keep stride with her. His hand reached into her hair, fingers snagging in the tresses like a net. He seized tight, and Talia's head snapped back. She yowled in surprise as her body jerked away from its course. He gripped her shoulders and thrust her to the ground. She struck the bottom steps hard and coughed in pain against the impact.

"Careful!" Lina hissed. "Don't damage her."

Lamont froze, looking at Lina before scooping Talia from the floor. The raging flight dissolved from Talia, replaced by a heavy, panicked remorse. She wanted to fall out of the back of her head and squeeze between the floorboards. Yet she remained trapped, in her flesh, in Lamont's clutches.

Holding her firm against his chest, he dragged her along the ground. The toes of her shoes skidded against the stairs. The muscled shape of Lamont's chest pressed firm against her shoulders, telling her how strong he was. This close to him, his scent filled her nose. She choked on the musty aroma of sweat mingled with a foreign spice. The edge of the smell bit at her nostrils as she sniffed through building sobs.

With Talia back under control, Lina nodded and moved into the red light, the first door to the left of the stairs. She disappeared into the open door, and something about her movement sent a spike of anxiety through Talia. She struggled to plant her feet and tug away from Lamont. His grip held fast on her arms, unmoving, as if he were holding a child through a tantrum. Her muscles burned, thin and acidic, yet they continued to pump and fight.

Against her back, Lamont's chest vibrated. His low voice rumbled in a lyrical chant of sharp syllables she could not identify. He repeated the melody like a sadistic lullaby as he marched her closer to the red light.

"Come on, Lamont," Lina called. "I'm hungry."

Hungry? Did she say hungry? Talia thought. She kicked her legs hard but lost all purchase on the floor. Lamont lifted her like a doll and lengthened his strides up the stairs.

As he turned toward the door, soft red light bathed over Talia. Her pupils contracted; her heart seized in her chest; her mind blanked into static. Her body panicked and flailed, yet she was far removed from it. There was that depersonalization again. Lamont carried her thrashing form effortlessly, while Talia seemed to watch it all from above.

Lina leaned her hip against a massive stone table. The rough-cut legs propped up the massive gray slab. Candelabras blazed on either side of her, casting shifting light and shadow over her arms. She held a small dagger in her hand and twirled the knife to let it dance in the light. Talia watched the spin of the blade in a terrible mesmerize.

"No no no no, please." Talia's voice returned like a habit, dribbling from her lips.

Lina and Lamont moved with the fluidity of giants ignoring an ant. Lamont cradled Talia like an inconsolable baby before dropping her on the stone slab. Lina pressed away from the table, continuing to toy with the blade, as Lamont wrapped thick leather straps around each of Talia's limbs.

With the last binding fastened, tears snaked out of Talia's eyes and spilled onto the stone table below.

She whimpered as she flexed against the leather straps. Her arms and legs flailed up from the slab, tensing the bindings before slapping back down in defeat. The more she struggled, the more the panic surged in her chest. Her fear animated her limbs more than her intention.

Having secured Talia into place, Lamont lumbered through the candlelight and red glow to recline on the far wall. He crossed his thick arms across his wide chest and rested his eyes comfortably on Talia, enjoying her waning fight.

Lina waited for him to settle, glancing from the sides of her eyes and smirking. Then she pushed to the edge of the table. She dragged the tip of her blade along the stone. It sent sharp ripples up through Talia, and her whimpers grew more desperate. Stopping, Lina gazed down at Talia's young face.

"I look old." Lina reached a hand toward her cheek.

"Never, *asynjur*," Lamont argued. "What's on the menu tonight?"

Lina's eyes flashed as her lips curled into a savage grin. "A special treat. I need to truly restore myself."

Talia's cries quieted as the two chatted. She flicked her eyes between them, straining to hear over the pulsation of her own terrified thoughts.

"Like those backpackers when we were in Tennessee?" Lamont asked.

Lina licked her lips in reflexive memory, her focus wobbling for an instant. Then her grin sharpened. "No." Her eyes sparkled in the candlelight. "More special, more vital than that. I need to fully replenish."

"Like those vagrants camping in our woods?"

She tipped her head and scowled. "That was reckless of us."

His eyebrow cocked as he tilted his head. "Have we had this before?"

Her smirk twitched. "We have not." She wandered across the floorboards to him, allowing her hand to trail his chest. "But I have. Back in the home country, long before I found you."

"What have we not had?" Lamont's eyes shot open as he leaned toward Lina.

Lina consumed his curiosity with a greedy tongue peeking from behind her teeth. Lamont watched the pink tip of muscle flick into view, then stared at her curled lips. Tipping his head around Lina, he lay his icy stare on Talia's wriggling form.

The stone pressed constant and aggressive into Talia's back. Her hair ground into the back of her skull as she writhed. Pressure points blossomed under her hips and shoulders where her body suddenly felt so heavy and worthless. Her mind whirred with fear, yet at the center of that hurricane, she fixated on her parents. Her vivid regret stabbed through all her panic to pierce her hammering heart.

Lina spun slowly to join Lamont's fixation on Talia. All four of their icy eyes burned into her. Talia flinched back from their hungry gaze, shrinking within the straps. Lamont took a heavy step toward the table.

"So, what are you taking? What is your treat?" he asked.

TEN

SATURDAY 3:38 A.M.

GLASS SHATTERED AGAINST the screwdriver, the crack splintering the night air. Autumn and Colin gasped at its volume. They hunkered together against the house. Yet the seconds ticked past uneventfully, with them holding their breath in the dark shadow.

Easing up, she peered through the broken glass. He leaned in behind her. Hearts hammering in sync, they peered through the ragged edges of the window. The neglected fire crackled in the fireplace, flames licking the remaining logs and casting moving light over the vacated couch and chair.

Rocking back on her heels and gripping the windowsill, Autumn poised to launch through the opening. Colin snatched her hips. She whipped burning copper eyes back at him. He held her, making an exaggerated show of pulling his sleeve over his hand. Clearing the remaining shards jutting out from the window frame, he stepped out of her way. Crouching, he laced his fingers as a boost.

The rage in Autumn stuttered and seized enough for a swell of affection to break through. She slid her hand onto Colin's shoulder, feeling its solid structure reassuring beneath her fingers. Briefly returning his soft grin, she planted her shoe into his grip.

On a desperate exhale, she dragged herself into Red Walls House. Glass crunched beneath her shoes as heat from the fire licked against her chilled cheeks. With her feet on the floorboards, she pulled out her gun, cupping her hands around it as she had practiced at the range so many times. Colin grunted behind her as he hoisted himself through the window.

They stood frozen on the shattered glass. He clutched her shoulder tight. She focused on the metal in her hand. Every muscle clenched as she throbbed in anticipation. She was ready to plow through and introduce herself. She was ready to release all the violence that had been brewing inside her for years.

She moved past the shifting flames and to the door. The floorboards creaked low below her. Colin's hand slid from her shoulder, yet he remained directly behind her, close enough for her to feel his heat.

The floor branched out into shadow. She hugged the wall, close enough to trace the rough wood as she approached the darkness. Her heart forced her pulse into her ears and eyes. Yet all she heard was her daughter's name throbbing through her veins. Tal-ia, Tal-ia on every throb of the muscle.

Talia.

Vomit burned up against the back of Autumn's molars. She flexed her throat against it and stumbled through the door. She staggered down the hall. At the stairs, she slowed and steadied herself on the thick banister.

The house was eerily quiet, the revelry of its occupants vanished. The abrupt stillness unsettled her.

"Where are they?" Colin voiced her worries.

She held up her hand and looked toward the entrance to the house.

"There's no way they didn't hear us break in," he continued behind her.

"So?" she whispered back. She wanted to find them. That was the whole point.

His breathing stuttered in answer. She gazed to the massive door, shrouded in odd, sharp shadows, then turned up the staircase, eyes tracing the banister stretching down. Like a tongue spilling from a dark maw.

Upstairs. Was upstairs the right way to go? Where had her baby's assailants gone? She rested against the railing for a breath, straining to hear over her slamming pulse. Deep in the nebulous above, there was a creak, a shuffle.

The sound blew on the coals of her rage, reignited her purpose. The gun sang a vengeful song to her, humming up her nerves to serenade her mind. Revenge, action rather than grief, was right there at the top of the stairs. She fought the impulse to sprint and tempered her ascent. Colin sighed hard as he trailed her.

The summit was dark and shapeless. The hall turned to the left and also stretched to the right. Autumn could not see the end of either direction. All the doors were shut tight, offering no light. Just an abyss poised to swallow them.

When Colin joined her, his shoulder brushed along her. She tried to hold her breath for another sound, an instinct, anything to direct her rage.

The sound started so low she assumed it was in her mind, but when the mewling whimper floated through the air again, her head snapped toward it. Colin turned with her, and they surged down the hall, past the first door on the left to the next.

The muttering and whining were distinctly human yet unintelligible, a sound just out of the reach of hearing. It left her mind groping at its shape as her eyes searched the darkness. The hall felt impossibly long until the murmurs snuck from below the door in front of them.

Her thoughts fluttered around her head, crashing into her skull. *Talia is home. Is someone else here? Are they hurting someone else?* They could do more than avenge Talia; they could save someone else tonight. Perhaps that would be enough to fill the hole left in her after Juni.

She reached for the doorknob, hand twitching around her gun. The door glided slowly into the room, lit low by candles. She pressed into the doorframe, peeking in, checking all corners.

"It's empty," she whispered to Colin.

And silent. The cries had vanished.

Keeping her gun ready, she shuffled in, scrutinizing the room. Colin joined her, keeping his back to hers as they spun.

A long wooden table extended down the first wall. The wood was thick, roughly finished. A gray fur spread over the top, and long metal swords lay atop it in neat lines, metal glinting. Sprinkled between the blades were small wolf and bear figures made of wood, metal, maybe even bone. A small wooden bowl cradled dry plants that quivered at their steps, pale petals red and veined with pointed leaves. At the far end of the table, a small, checkered wooden tablet held carved pawns. One brown piece sat surrounded by white figures.

Several spears and a great axe propped against the wall. When Autumn took a step back, she saw the shields mounted above. The metal one gleamed, a design of sharp angles carved into its center. She leaned forward, squinting, and saw indentions near the edge of the shield. Small lines forming a familiar crescent. A bite mark?

The other was plank wood, cut into a circle with a metal plate pointing out from its center. A small circular symbol was scratched into the wall below. One line bisected it with two lines creating downward points across.

Lowering his gun to his side, Colin wandered along the table, staring at its contents, then the shields.

"*Skjaldmær?*" he murmured.

"What?" she whispered.

He shook his head and continued down the table.

Turning away from him to take in the rest of the room, she startled.

The beast loomed in the corner, its dull black eyes staring lifeless. In the grave shadows, the draped bearskin appeared ferocious. The massive head propped atop a wooden stand, and the fur poured down behind it. The grizzly mouth froze in a snarl, revealing vicious white teeth and an arched pink tongue. The black eyes held wide, reflecting the candles and Autumn's face as she leaned closer.

Colin joined her fascination. Mesmerized, he stepped forward and ran his hand along the bristled fur.

"*Bjorn.*" The woman's voice shattered the silence.

Colin startled from his stupor, stumbling against the bear and nearly toppling the stand. He groped at the massive head to steady it before turning wild eyes to the woman who seemed to have appeared in the room. She crossed her arms loose and casual across her stomach, an amused smirk curling her lips.

"The bear is beautiful, no?" Her smile grew as she took a menacing step forward. "Though I think he was quieter than the two of you barreling through my window."

Autumn's mind blanked at the sight of her. The woman's pale skin against the black lace, her towering height crowned with blonde braids, eyes as sharp as shards of glass. Then Autumn's thoughts found their footing, and she raised the gun.

Before she could squeeze the trigger, the woman's cold hand was around her wrist, as unyielding as stone. The woman stripped the gun from her grip, smiling in Autumn's face. Autumn could have sworn the woman's eyes had faded to white. Then, in a blur of fair hair, the woman was gone.

With the gun.

Autumn's hand gaped around the vacancy. Her fingers flexed at the phantom of her weapon. The gun she had practiced with all those years ago. The metal that made her feel empowered and prepared, safe.

The woman flitted out of the door like an apparition. So fleeting and shocking that Autumn would have thought her a hallucination if her gun was not gone with her. The woman had been so fast. Inhumanly fast.

An instinct tugged to give chase, to retrieve her weapon and use it to execute her purpose. Yet she was rattled. Something about the brief exchange had turned her skin inside out, leaving her mind less pointed and her heart less convicted. An urge more basic than words clamored in warning.

Colin stepped up to pull her against his body. His gun wavered slightly as he pointed it at the door.

"Shit," he gasped. "How did she do that?"

"S-s-something's not right," Autumn managed.

Colin swallowed an *I told you so,* but it floated in the air between them.

The woman's icy eyes had cooled Autumn's rage, smoldered the fire that had been stoking her frenzy. *What am I doing?* she thought. Had she really thought she could leave her child in bed and come murder the people who hurt her? How did she really think this was all going to go? Her murderous fantasies had always ended with the life draining out of that drunk bastard's eyes. Even if they had planned for after, she had only fixated on the act.

It had never included whatever had just plucked her gun from her as if she were a feeble child.

The cold hand wrapping around her heart suggested they should get out of there, abandon this revenge fantasy, return to their daughter. Now.

"We have to get back to Talia," she said, low into Colin's beard.

"We can still just go," he said. "Let's go."

He stepped in front of her, crouching, trailing his arm to keep her close. Even with the knives folded in her pocket, she was naked and vulnerable, unprepared. She pinched his shirt between her fingers as she chased him back into the dark hall.

He pivoted back toward the steps and marched without a second glance. Singular focus toward retreat. She let his shirt guide her as she scanned the walls. When they approached the next room, the door now hung ajar. Red light spilled out and splashed over the hallway floorboards. It menaced; it beckoned. She could not resist peeking.

More candles flickered low, contributing little to the dim red light. In the center of the room, a massive stone table consumed most of the floor. The candles outlined the room with trinkets and bundles of dried leaves spliced in between. When she spied the small puddle on the table, she halted, releasing Colin's shirt.

The light would make any liquid look like blood in this room, but she knew. Her child's blood sang to her, calling the shared cells in her own veins. Without a thought, she detoured toward the table.

Colin managed a few paces before he noticed her absence. "Autumn," he called from far away.

The table commanded attention. She wanted to shrink away from it as much as she was drawn to place her palms on its surface. The blood insisted. She put her hands to the stone. The sensation of the surface sent a shock along her nerves. Closing her eyes, she hung her head and choked on a breath.

When she opened her eyes, they wandered the table. In the low light, she glimpsed the leather straps left unbuckled at each end. She stopped breathing. She touched the straps with trembling fingers, the buckles scratching the stone at her touch. Tears returned hot to her eyes as she gripped the leather in one hand and the room dissolved around her.

"What do we have here?" The gruff voice shattered the silence, booming from behind Autumn.

She startled, snatching her hands into her chest and whirling her back into the table. She pressed hard into the stone until she could feel the patterns leaving indentions in her flesh.

The bald man consumed the doorway, reclining on a raised arm in casual amusement. His other arm wrapped around Colin's throat like a constricting snake. Colin struggled silently while the man ran his cold eyes over Autumn unbothered. She stood frozen, her mind blanked by panic. The man pushed away from the frame and took a step toward her. She flinched but could not sink through the table.

"Those eyes." He squinted and waved a thick finger toward her face. "I know those eyes." A grin bunched up his mustache and ruffled his beard. "You must be her mother."

ELEVEN
FRIDAY 11:59 P.M.

THE ENERGY IN the red room changed. *Treat?* What did they mean treat? Talia was not sure she wanted to let the possibilities tread on her mind. She held her breath.

Lina swished past Lamont, the lace of her dress licking along the floor. As she drew closer to Talia, her breathing changed, deepening and growling. Lamont took on a similar rumble. Talia's skin contracted in gooseflesh at the sound, her eyes flitting between the two.

They loomed over Talia for an insufferable moment. Then Lina's hand darted out and snatched the hem of Talia's shirt, yanking it up to expose her trembling stomach. Gasping and instinctively sucking in her belly, Talia wished she could press herself down through the stone.

Treat.

As Lina and Lamont glared down at Talia's exposed skin, their eyes grew paler, fading from blue to near white. The irises disappeared into the orbs of their eyes, leaving only ravenous pupils dilating in the center, spreading like ink. Releasing the shirt, Lina swept her hands over Talia's body.

Talia cowered, waiting for the hand to grab, grope, violate. Instead, Lina teased just above the flesh. Where Talia could feel her heat but not her touch. The fingers hovering over Talia's stomach twitched and cracked. With each unnatural jerk, the fingernails elongated and jutted farther from the fingertip. They formed white spires with terrifying, looming points. Once they had fully extracted, the fingers fell into still levitation again.

Lina lowered her index finger toward Talia. Talia's belly spasmed with her frightened breaths. Lina grinned at the sound of Talia's panic, watching her own nail descend. She planted the tips of her fingers below Talia's ribs, then dragged them down, catching and tugging at the skin.

The pain ripped through Talia, drawing vivid lines from Lina's nails screaming up her nerves. Her thoughts tore away, and her fear consolidated down to the sensations. She was here. She was perched on what was going to happen to her. She chomped down onto her lip and the sobs building behind it.

Lamont leaned closer, his white eyes widening. His scent packed into Talia's nostrils. Every breath was saturated in his anticipation for whatever Lina had in store. His excitement vibrated the air that tasted like him. Talia wanted to vomit the flavor out of her mouth, her diaphragm contracting around the impulse.

Lina raked over Talia's skin until the touch blurred. Then, abruptly, she gripped the waist of Talia's pants and tore the button free. Talia gasped hard at the exposure and pinched her eyes shut, sending tears spilling down her cheeks. The air on tender flesh made her feel so naked, so vulnerable.

No no no no no no, she chanted in her mind.

The tears surfaced in Talia's eyes in waves. Her sinuses flooded, and she sniffed back, drowning as she looked to the red ceiling. Her lips quivered. She tried to force breaths, yet the cries racked her ribs. The length of her exposed skin shook, waiting for them.

"Are you toying with her or me?" Lamont's voice came out as a growl.

Lina whipped around to him, her blonde waves spiraling behind her. She retracted her hand from Talia long enough to trace her nails over his bald scalp. A sinister smile cut across her face as his eyes fluttered shut.

Talia wrinkled her nose at their exchange. In their distraction, she gave the straps another futile tug. The seconds Lina and Lamont focused on each other stretched into eternity.

Then their attention returned to her.

"Are you ready?" Lina said to Lamont, her focus back on Talia.

Talia sucked her belly in away from Lina's elongated nails. Lamont placed his hands to the stone beside Talia's thigh, crouching in close. He opened his mouth so that his rasping breaths grew louder. Then his tongue spilled out. The thick pink muscle stretched and thinned, turning gray as it formed a sharp fork at the end. Talia blinked hard as she strangled on her own breath.

The room froze. All three stopped breathing. Lina lifted her nail high, holding it above Talia. They all stared at the tip as it trembled in suspense.

Lina's arm struck in a flash. The nail sank into Talia, plunging into the tender flesh at the curve of her hip. Talia shrieked against the vivid penetration, arching her back and driving the nail even deeper. She flopped back against the stone in a whimper.

The finger disappeared into Talia's belly. Angling over it, Lina smiled into the pressure. Blood blossomed from the wound like a terrible fountain. It poured over Talia's skin, warm and awful. Lamont leaned forward. His long tongue extended and lapped around the tear. A gag seized Talia's throat before she released another scream the room ignored.

Lamont's tongue chased the nail as it opened Talia like a zipper. His lapping drew burning wriggles at the edges of Talia's parted flesh. Her nerves shrieked in a cacophony, an off-key symphony of pain. They drew barbed, flashing shapes in her mind. She felt everything and nothing at the same time. Her body stuttered, struggling to remember how to breathe.

Her eyes rolled back in their sockets, dissolving her sight into a panicked red. She became only the chaotic screaming pain screeching over her. Her entire belly exploded in the sensation as it yawned in the wound, spreading far beyond the breadth of her flesh. She wanted to keep yelling yet chomped down on her bottom lip, bit through it to contain the pointless sounds.

She tugged at her restraints until her hands and feet faded into memory.

Lamont's eyes and mouth shadowed Lina's finger, ravenous. The flow of blood slipping past his maw mesmerized Lina. Her white eyes gaped. Talia's flesh unfolded as if releasing years of strung tension. The layers of skin, thin bit of fat, fibers of muscle separated and opened the deep cavity.

Letting in dim, red light where it was never supposed to see.

Talia swam in her misery above them, slipping beneath the surface as the vivid edge of the room around her blurred.

Once Lina opened a gruesome, bleeding hole along Talia's hip, she retracted the nail. As she curled her fingers toward her face, blood splattered back on Talia. Talia coughed and sputtered in a strangled relief, going limp against the stone. Lamont slurped up the blood flowing over Talia's hip before craning up.

Talia gaped at them. Lamont and Lina locked white eyes. Blood dripped bright from Lamont's pallid face. Droplets crawled down through his wiry goatee. His bare scalp gleamed in the flickering candlelight. Lina wiggled her savage nails and unleashed a slicing smile. Her face curved and contorted inhumanely in the grimace.

"I'm sorry." The words dribbled incoherently from Talia's lips. Her eyelids draped low. "I'm sorry, Mom. I'm sorry, Dad." Tears snuck from beneath her lashes and fled down her cheeks as her head lolled from side to side.

Sliding her hands along Talia's legs, Lina brought her elongated nails to each side of the gaping wound. Her fingers toyed with the ragged edges for a breath, letting the skin bounce and flap wetly. Then she plunged into the flesh. Gasping, Talia's eyes snapped wide, and her back tensed hard. Torn muscles that could not contract. A shaking, broken body.

Lina's long tongue escaped to flit wildly around her lips as she concentrated. Wrist deep in Talia's abdomen, she pulled and stretched at the wound. Talia dissolved into feral howls and desperate writhing. Lina was ripping her in half. She could feel her body coming apart.

Yet Lina was immune to the protest. She concentrated hard as she slipped her hand into the cavity, crouching close enough for her exhalations to brush along Talia's skin. As if Talia could feel anything over the trauma. The tendons in Lina's arm rolled and flexed as she dug around inside Talia.

Until she seized her target.

Her face, her movements changed. Her determination softened, melted into a twisted joy, and she withdrew her hand with care. As it pulled out of Talia, Lina sliced at dangling connective tissue with her other hand, closing her fingers around the small organ. She clutched it close, almost tenderly, as she brought it to her chest and stepped back from the stone table.

Lina pinched the small, round organ between her nails. The lumpy white flesh branched in fragile red veins. She stared at it enamored as her tongue teased at the curves of its shape.

Cold sweat prickled over Talia's skin. Her limbs flopped limp and quivering against the stone. Razored sensations flooded over her nerves in waves, causing her hair follicles to stretch in painful gooseflesh. She licked at her lips, yet her tongue felt like sandpaper and offered no moisture. Her bottom lip throbbed. No matter how she gulped at the thick air, she still heaved out of breath. Her eyes swam through the low, shifting light in the room. When they did finally snatch focus, Lina loomed over her.

Blue irises resurfaced from the white orbs of Lina's eyes and nearly glowed down at Talia in their intensity. Talia hated the piercing sensation of the contact, how it felt like more of a violation than Lina's hand digging around inside her abdomen.

Lina planted a hand beside Talia's head. Talia shimmied futilely as Lina eased over her. Lina drew blood-slicked fingers along Talia's face. The nails had begun to recede into a more human appearance as they clutched the fleshy bulb.

Talia turned to the organ in Lina's grasp. Her eyes widened in horror as it permeated her mind that she was looking at *her* blood on Lina's fingers, *her* body part in Lina's hand. A blur of anatomy diagrams and half-attended lessons whirred through her mind as she reeled to identify the piece of her. She concentrated so hard she forgot to breathe.

"What's the matter, little lamb?" Lina offered a vicious smile. "Did you not stay in school long enough to learn what this is?" She brought the organ close to Talia's face, forcing her to examine it.

"This is your ovary, half of your fertility in my hand." She looked to the ovary. "And all its potential."

Lina drew the ovary back and brought it to her mouth. Parting her lips slowly, she extended her tongue to unfurl and tease around her meal. She stared down into Talia as she sank her teeth through the flesh. The satisfaction dripped from her features while she savored it. The sight only nauseated Talia. Her mind scrabbled around what was happening, unable to find a hold.

Lina moaned with pleasure and turned back to Lamont. "This will make me feel 100 years younger," she cooed. "Not only can I taste this piece of her life but all the possible lives inside it."

Lamont watched her feast, glancing between Lina's bloodied lips and Talia's gaping abdomen. His eyes stretched hungrily. "And is that all?"

"We cannot be careless again," Lina dismissed. "She has spilled plenty of blood for you."

Lamont's face slackened and he stared at her. "She has other duplicate organs."

Savagery sparkled in Lina's face as she turned her shoulders toward him. She waited, inviting him to wilt. He kept his mouth shut but did not surrender her gaze. Finally, she shrugged with a chuckle.

"I supposed another morsel could not hurt. There is something about her flavor." Lina's eyes rolled down to Talia. "Get me a jar. We will save it for later. Would you prefer a lobe of her pickled liver or one of her toxic kidneys?"

"Liver," he grinned.

"I am unsurprised." Lina flicked her razor nail out and leaned back over Talia.

Talia did not even feel Lina shuffling and slicing at her innards. Sensation had abandoned her. Her mind fled her flesh, wrapping itself in flickering figments of the night that brought her here. When Lina retracted a slab of dark meat from inside her, for an instant, it was comically surreal. This was someone else's body, someone else's death.

Lina presented the flesh to Lamont, and he lifted the empty glass jar to meet her. Sliding the liver lobe inside, she took the jar in slick hands. As she seated the lid, she eased out of his way. In her wake, Lamont dove down, slapping his palms on either side of Talia.

His tongue plunged into the wound. Talia managed a thrashing moan, yet no longer pulled against the straps. The darkness on the edges of her sight dilated thicker. Lamont's long and thick tongue slithered frantically along the opening, a soft sizzle tracing its movements. The blood flow slowed, then ceased. As Lamont's mouth moved over her skin, the wound drew closed. The vile cauterization stitched her back together. His tongue ran along edges, burning them together in a raised, brown line.

Joining him, Lina closed her eyes and licked her lips, her tongue shortening and turning pink once more. She faced Talia again. "Don't worry." Softening, she placed a hand on either side of Talia's face. "You still have one more. You are already healed. You can return to your vagrant life with nothing more than a hangover and a story no one will believe."

New adrenaline surged through Talia. Her muscles tensed past the pain. She released a savage scream, something that came from deep inside of her, somewhere below where they had been rummaging around, into Lina's face. The sound shook her molars, yet Lina stood unaffected. When Talia flopped back against the table, Lina cracked a bemused grin and licked her bloody fingers. The elongated nails had retreated entirely back into their human length.

A different pain roiled through Talia under her physical sensations. Rage bubbled up from the void in her abdomen and sizzled through her until it exploded in her mind.

"Fuck you," Talia coughed, the words pointed like daggers.

"What's that, little lamb?" Lina lowered her frigid eyes.

"FUCK YOU!" Talia unleashed the words, flailing wildly in her bindings. "You psychos! You assholes! Fuck you!" She thrashed as the words disintegrated out of her cries.

Lina's face hardened, her features going severe in the candlelight. She stepped back from the table with her nose wrinkling as Lamont stomped up behind her. Talia thrust her arms against the straps with abandon, ignoring the burn permeating her muscles.

She ignored her entire body. She ignored Lamont menacing over her.

She felt only the rage.

"What are you going to do, you cunts? You cannibal fucks!" Talia forced her eyes to meet Lamont's, though his gaze chilled her.

Lamont glowered down at Talia, his mustache bristling above his pursed lips. He slapped Talia, the weight of his hand shaking her eyeballs in their sockets. A new detonation of pain ignited Talia's cheek and silenced her. She gulped and sucked at her lip until she tasted blood.

Talia dropped her head to the table and felt vibration through the stone. From beneath all her pain, she struggled to identify it. When it buzzed again, she realized the source was in her back pocket.

Lina and Lamont moved forward, exchanging narrow glances. Lina wriggled her hands under Talia to extract the quivering phone. She tilted the glowing screen to Lamont.

"Mom?" Lamont glared at the phone before flicking his eyes to Lina, then Talia.

Talia tensed, her mouth wide enough to swallow her captors. Her mother was looking for her. In every cell of her body, she could feel how much she wanted to be held by her mother.

I should have stayed home. Why didn't I just stay home? The thoughts returned with the tears. The guilt hurt more than her body.

"I thought she was a vagrant," Lamont spoke into Lina's ear.

Lina continued to stare at the phone until it stopped seizing.

Mom is going to be freaking out now, Talia thought, her heartrate climbing.

"She certainly looked like it, drunk and dirty, stumbling by herself at night." Lina glanced down at Talia, then back to the dark device. "No one comes here at night." She touched a bloody finger to her forehead. "Perhaps we are losing touch with this age."

"What do we do now?"

"We have to release her as planned. If she were to go missing, there would be too many…" Lina tongued her lips slow. "Questions. Remember what happened after our feast in the woods."

"And what if she tells her mother?"

Lina placed the phone, screen down, beside Talia, looking hard into her eyes. "Who would believe such a fantastical story from a drunk little girl? Right, little lamb?" Lina slithered over Talia, her hair dangling to brush Talia's cheeks. "Because if your mother did believe, if people did come looking, I would hate to eat their hearts." She hesitated, cocked her head. "Do you understand?"

Talia burrowed her skull back into the stone, blinking stunned at Lina.

Getting out of here? Am I getting out of here?

Nothing else mattered. Any agreement was worth it. She could bury this night like a fevered dream and never speak of it again if it meant she could hug her parents tonight.

Lina's lips turned in a thin grin, and she popped up from the table. "I really wouldn't hate to eat them, but I think we understand each other." She nodded to Lamont. "Turn her loose."

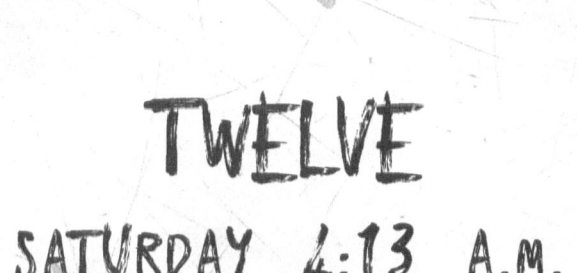

TWELVE
SATURDAY 4:13 A.M.

"Monsters?" Willow sputtered. "Talia, you're just upset."

"We have to go save them." Talia sharpened and sprang from the mattress, blowing past her friends and to her closet.

"What the fuck do you mean, save them?" Ricky gaped after her.

With a hoodie clutched in her hands, Talia turned back and just stared at them. Then she thrust it over her head. When she emerged from the hood, her features were resolute. Ricky glanced to Willow.

"What are you waiting for?" Talia shouted.

"Tal, calm down." Willow rose from the bed. "We just don't understand. We—"

"You're talking about fucking monsters!" Ricky shouted and threw his hands. "You sound *loco*. Crazy."

"Ricky!" Willow scolded.

Talia froze and lifted her face to them. Tears drew tracks down her cheeks. Gripping the hem of her shirt, she exposed her stomach. The bruises, the scratches, and that thick cauterized line.

That silenced them. Willow's jaw dropped, and Ricky lowered back to the bed.

"They took it," Talia managed. The words were clunky and uncomfortable in her mouth. She chewed the welling sob to get them out.

"Took what?" Ricky's voice was low, tenuous. Willow remained stunned.

The cry choked its way out of Talia. She wrapped around it, dropping her shirt, though it still felt like she was displaying her injuries. "My ovary." The name tasted horrible, vile, like loss. "And part of my liver."

"Oh my God," Willow breathed, clasping her hands over her mouth. She gripped until she left fingerprints on her cheeks.

"Your—" Ricky coughed into his hand. "Ovary?"

"How? How?" Willow hitched on the word. "How do you know?"

Talia winced and hiccupped more tears. "She showed it to me."

Talia wilted into the silence of the room. Ricky and Willow looked at her, then back at each other. Ricky rose to his feet, stiff with clenched and shaking fists.

"Let's go," he said. Willow snatched at his wrist, but he shook her off. "No, let's go handle this. And save your parents."

He moved to Talia and took her shoulders, drawing her into him. She collapsed into his chest, letting him hold her. For just an instant.

"Go save her parents? How the hell are we going to do that?" Willow said from the bed. "How are we going to save your parents from monsters? We need to tell someone. We need to get help."

A sour chuckle fractured Talia's soft weeping. She turned her face to Ricky, and he smirked in reply. Willow looked between the two of them.

"Like who, Lo?" Ricky tipped his head. "My mother is drowning in my brothers and sisters, won't even know I'm gone. Your parents?"

"My parents are flower children." She shook her head. "No cops, no violence." An idea lighted on her face. "What about the party? Isn't everyone at Devon's?"

Ricky's wrist fell limp as he squinted. "You want to storm Red Walls House with a band of drunken teenagers?"

Willow deflated. Squeezing Talia's shoulders again, Ricky released her to finish getting changed. As she removed her pajamas, she could feel their eyes mapping out her damaged flesh. She could not cover herself fast enough.

"What are they, Tal?" Willow had not left the mattress, now wringing her hands.

"I don't know." Talia tugged on her jeans and pulled on socks.

"Are they just cannibals?" Willow asked.

"No," Talia snapped, cracking nails and long tongues slashing through her mind. "No, they were different. They changed."

Willow flinched back and raised her hands. "I don't understand," she said to her lap.

"What do we need?" Ricky asked. "Your parents seemed pretty prepared."

Talia rubbed her hands along her braids, hanging her head. Lina's white eyes greeted her when she blinked. Her own dripping organ hovered over her face. Lamont's greedy tongue sizzled as it lapped up her blood.

Somehow, that cold slab under her trembling body became dark asphalt, shards of glass catching the light of passing cars. Her mother's voice pierced the night as Talia stared at the small bloody hand peeking out from beneath the white sheet.

Screaming. Her mother screaming. Wailing from the past to harmonize with how Talia imagined she was crying right now. In that house. Was she on that awful altar, awash with red light? Was her father? Had Lina and Lamont eaten them already, sparing them the grace of release?

It was all her fault.

"Talia!" Ricky called.

Talia jumped, nearly blinded by her memories. Ricky raised his hands as she blinked fast and swiped at her cheeks.

"Can we go now?" Talia's eyes bounced around the room, avoiding Ricky and Willow.

Willow drew up on her knees. Ricky placed his hands on Talia again, shushing softly. He looked over his shoulder at Willow and jerked his head.

"Yeah, we can go now," Ricky said. "You tell us what we need to do."

Talia whirled around, searching for her shoes. Stooping, Ricky extracted one from under her bed. He extended it to her and offered a gentle smile when she took it.

Talia's body ached as she rushed. She burst from the front door first, her friends trailing behind her. Tromping onto the lawn, she looked between the two cars hastily parked in front of her house.

"Whose car are we taking?" she asked.

Her parents were adamant about not giving Talia her own car. After Juni.

Willow stopped on the grass, holding herself. "I don't know if I can. I—" Her eyes shifted from side to side, avoiding them both.

"Excuse us just a minute." Ricky gave Talia a pursed smile and snatched Willow by the arm, dragging her across the driveway.

"Ow! Ricky!"

He pulled her to the other side of the yard, but Talia could still hear them. She turned away and nibbled her nail to pretend she wasn't paying attention.

"What the fuck is wrong with you?" Ricky's whisper was harsh and sharp on the edges.

"What is wrong with me? *This.*" She gestured around wildly. "This is what's wrong with me. This is too much. Too dangerous." She pursed her lips. "Too scary."

Ricky lowered his chin and his voice. "They hurt her, Lo. And Autumn and Colin are there now. What if something happens to them? Talia would be all alone."

"What can we possibly do?" She tossed her arms and retreated a step. "If it is like she says."

They both cast a glance to Talia as she rocked impatiently in the yard.

"We just have to be there," Ricky said. "It has been the three of us since sixth grade. You were there for Juni, when my father ran off, everything. You have to be here now. Do you want her going alone? You know she is going either way."

Wilting on a sigh, Willow shook her head.

"I didn't think so." Ricky smirked, then returned to serious. "You've been there for her since the beginning." He squeezed her shoulder. "Don't stop now."

Placing a gentle hand on her back, he guided her to Talia. Fishing the keys from his pocket, he dangled them on his finger before snapping his hand shut around them.

"We're taking my car," he said.

THIRTEEN

AUTUMN WATCHED THE pale woman snatch Colin from the man and throw him into the red light with alarming strength. The man pinned Autumn against the stone table, seizing her wrists in one of his massive hands. The grip felt like a stone manacle to match the table.

Lamont smelled earthy, musty. The way Autumn would imagine the woods or a wild animal would smell. Despite the cornucopia of frights before her eyes, the odor insisted on captivating her. The smell was not bad or rank. It was just so pungent, earthen.

Colin stumbled into the table, landing at Autumn's feet.

"Colin!" she cried as she tugged against Lamont's unmoving hands.

"The parents?" Lamont leaned toward Lina, pushing Autumn aside.

Looking them over, Lina hummed agreement. "It is so rare that the prey comes to you. The little lamb must have cried." She leaned down to run a finger over Colin's sweaty scalp, bringing it to her nose. "This one looks like home." She dipped her finger into her mouth. "Maybe that is why the lamb was so sweet. Something nostalgic in the blood."

Autumn found distraction in Lamont's odor and in Lina's pale eyes. The eyes appeared to be blanching from their icy blue. It seemed like her iris would disappear at any moment.

"You don't think this could be a trap?" Lamont asked.

Lina reached out and ran her hand along his beard. He leaned into it like a cat. "Ever the strategist." She smiled without the edges. "They were so noisy, so sloppy. If they had gone to the authorities, they would not have broken into our home alone. You know how they all fear this place."

"As they should," he rumbled.

"But this does…complicate things." Lina plucked Colin from the ground, pushing him up beside Autumn.

"They have to die."

"Yes." Lina's eyes faded closer to white.

"What about the girl?"

Autumn's heart stopped at his mention of Talia. Of her girl. Of her last girl.

The sinister curl returned to Lina's lips. "I think she'll come back."

"Leave our daughter alone!" Colin shouted from the floor, his voice and the volume startling Autumn. "You have done enough."

Lamont offered him a boot to the chest to silence him. Tipping her head, Lina crouched down to him. She pinched his chin between her long nails and turned him to her.

"We have not even begun." Glaring at him, she rose to tower over him. "But you will see."

Yanking Autumn from the table, Lamont hefted her over his shoulder in one movement. A strange sound escaped her lips as she lifted through the air. With her hands liberated, she used them to beat at his back. It felt like punching a rock. The obscenities she spit didn't matter.

Lina did not even reach for Colin. She flicked her finger at him, instructing him onto the stone. He looked at her, then along her pointed nail, but remained unmoved. His disobedience only caused her grin to carve deeper.

The stone knocked the air from Autumn as Lamont thrust her to the table. Her head rang for an instant after it bounced from the impact. She clutched at it but kicked her legs at him in every direction. Chuckling, he snatched her ankles and slammed them down hard enough to make her howl.

Her fight faded at the flare of pain. She could not wrench her mind from their words. They were going to kill them and wait for Talia. She had not saved her daughter at all, only damned her.

But maybe she would see Juni again.

That thought nearly broke her. She wanted to wrap up in the idea and sink below this room, find darkness until it became light. Then Colin flopped down beside her and brought her back.

"Hmmm, not enough straps." Lina poked her chin and giggled over them.

"I guess I'll have to get creative." Lamont smirked.

He departed for a terrible minute, leaving them rigid in awful anticipation as Lina grinned down at them. Her eyes glittered like she knew. He returned with a length of cord circling one shoulder and what looked like a massive needle.

"What is that?" she asked.

"It's a spike." He dropped the rope and stroked the long metal object.

"I can see that. What do you intend to do with it?"

"I once used it to thread rope through thick sails." His eyes sparked at the memory.

Forming a pleased o with her lips, she stepped out of the way.

He approached Colin with unnerving excitement. Looming over him, Lamont threaded the cord through the rough eye at the end of the spike. He seized Colin's wrist, planting the tip of the spike in the center of his palm.

Crucifixion imagery bombarded Autumn's brain. "No! No, leave him alone."

No one listened. Even Colin was bug-eyed and absorbed in what was coming.

Running his thin gray tongue along his whiskers, Lamont smiled and leaned into the spike. Colin's scream shook Autumn, vibrating her ears and freeing the tears trapped behind her nose. Blood gushed from Colin's hand. Leaning hard, Lamont dug the tip deeper and wriggled it in a circle. The spike chewed through his palm, struggled out the other side.

Colin's cries did not stop. Sweat beaded on his bare scalp, and his eyes swam in their sockets. Gagging, he heaved in his breaths.

Lamont forced the point past the flesh, lifting Colin's hand to show the tip piercing through. Then, as if sewing, he pulled the cord. Autumn could not process her disbelief, her horror. Colin trembled and sputtered beside her. Calmly, almost pacified, Lamont wound the bloody cord around Colin's other wrist, then tied it off under the table.

Lamont's twisted maw shifted to Autumn. Thrashing her legs, she wailed as if anyone cared. Lina seemed to lap it up as she observed from against the wall.

The pain was more than Autumn could fathom. Her hand was on fire until the spike pulled through, like a contraction during childbirth. Seizing in agony before releasing to its sweating, shaking wake. The fight fell out of her as Lamont lashed the ends to the table.

"You could have just bound their wrists." Lina laughed.

Lamont shrugged, beard puckering on his pleased smirk.

With them both secure and their shrieks shrinking to whimpers, Lina hovered over them. "Did you really think you would come avenge her?" She sang in a melody of condescension, the way one would talk to a foolish child. "Have you not heard the rumors of this place? Everyone has."

"Fuck you," Autumn spat, grimacing hard enough to grind her teeth. "You hurt my baby."

"Your baby was delicious!" Lina snapped in her face, her tongue wiggling to escape her lips.

Autumn clamored in rage and tugged at her binding, reigniting her pain. Angry, pained cries surged from her lips.

"She was home with you." Lina pushed her elbow into Colin's thigh, then propped her head on her hands. "You had her back. She could have gone on to live a normal life." A cackle erupted from her. "She probably would have even been able to still have children."

Autumn's veins ran cold as she pictured the welted scar across her daughter's belly. Colin grunted in the same agony beside her, but she nearly forgot him, glaring into Lina's eyes. She hated how much Lina was enjoying her suffering, but she could not stop providing it to her.

"Oh, she didn't tell you." Lina covered her mouth. "Good little lamb. But who did you tell?"

She moved closer to examine Autumn. Seeing nothing in her face, she turned back to Lamont.

"This place is expired, anyway." She shrugged. "Everyone around has heard of the Red Walls House on Monere Lane." She raised her hands to mock the words, rolling her eyes. She turned to her prey. "You can only stay ageless somewhere for so long. Eventually, they trace the bodies to you." She flipped her hand before placing a nail between her teeth. "But don't worry; they won't find you. Any of you."

Rage sizzled through Autumn. She wanted to scream, but those sounds had lost purpose. She wanted to cry, but these monsters would only savor her tears.

She wanted Talia, but her mind could only chant that her fledgling attempt at vengeance was going to cost them all.

Colin rocked his thigh against the table, grazing hers. The sweet touch on her skin contradicted all the pain garbling on her nerves. The sensation reminded her that he was there, that she was not alone in this misery. Rolling her head on the stone, she met his wobbling eyes.

The pain reflected there made her want to give up and also tear free to burn it all down.

"I cannot decide what smells sweeter," Lina said to Lamont. "His fear or her rage."

Lamont ran his tongue over a greedy smile. It did not look like a normal tongue. Not pink, not thick. Autumn and Colin gaped at the sharp point flicking around his mouth.

"This is going to be a true feast." Lamont tucked his tongue behind his words.

"We wanted to revitalize. We wanted to prepare for our relocation." Lina sauntered over to him. "The old gods delivered."

"The old gods," he scoffed.

She chuckled low. "I know, but it has a ring to it." She extended her sharp fingers and ran them over Colin, then Autumn's legs, scratching and tearing at the fabric.

"We haven't emptied one since being in this place."

Lina drew her nails over Autumn's shoe, raking over the sole, then up Lamont's arm. He did not cringe at the points of her nails.

Instead, his face softened. Autumn and Colin shared a confused glance before turning sick fascination to the end of the table.

Lina cradled Lamont's beard. "You have behaved so well, and we have waited long enough."

"A whole family," he mused. "A feast to rival the battlefields."

The monsters both snapped their attention to Autumn and Colin. Autumn strained against her bondage, cowering toward Colin until the pain restrained her.

"Let's prepare," Lina said. "We have plenty of time as we wait for the little lamb to come back to us."

FOURTEEN

RICKY TURNED HIS car onto Monere Lane.

"Monster Lane," Willow whispered, her eyes fixed on the street sign.

Talia's heart clenched, as if her chest was caving in. Devon's party felt like a lifetime ago. Her stumble onto this very asphalt felt like it happened to someone else. And anything beyond that, she wanted to forget.

If only she had lied better, concealed better, her parents would not be in Red Walls House. Why had she told them anything?

If only she had not gone alone to drown her memories in a bottle, none of them would be here. She could have mourned her sister with her parents in the same somber evening as every year. She could have listened to Ricky and Willow bicker over a movie.

Instead, they rolled over the spot where her nightmare began and drove toward the structure where she lost parts of herself.

They're okay, she told herself. *They have to be okay. I have to make this right.*

She repeated the thoughts over and over in her mind, trying to wear the points on her anxiety down, as the headlights spawned shadows through the forest.

"There's your parents' car." Ricky pulled up behind the vehicle.

Willow trembled in the back seat. Her quaking fingers clutched the back of Talia's headrest. Talia's mind acknowledged her but could not care. She was fixated on the looming house just through the trees. She felt it in her injuries, setting her nervous system alight in the worst color.

Red.

Yet she led the way. Her steps landed somewhere between impatient and reluctant. Ricky and Willow fumbled behind her, nearly as sloppy as Talia's panicked sprint through these trees. She thought she saw the tree she had tried to hide in, but all the dead fall looked the same in the dark.

"Willow, come on!" Ricky hissed.

Talia stopped on the next boulder and turned back to them. Willow practically glowed in the dying moonlight, her eyes bulging and messy bun bobbing. She could not look more uncomfortable. Talia had only seen her like this when embarrassed at school, especially in the shadow of her unconventional parents.

Huffing, Ricky pushed his hand against a tree trunk, side eyeing Willow then looking to Talia.

"You good?" Ricky asked her.

Talia nodded.

"You're not good." Willow smirked.

Talia scoffed. "No, I am not," she said to the forest floor. "I don't know how to be farther from okay."

Ricky nodded to Talia, and she turned to their final ascent. When they broke the trees, Red Walls House rose before them. It towered between the trunks, large and ominous enough to blot out the retreating moon.

Willow moved up beside Talia, grasping her fingertips. "Why do they call it Red Walls House? It's brown."

Ricky took Talia's other hand. "I always thought it meant hookers."

"Of course you did. That's a red light." Willow rolled her eyes.

Talia saw the red light bathing that terrible room and its altar. Her own red blood flowed freely over Lina's hand and into Lamont's mouth.

"Trust me." She squeezed both their hands. "It's the right name."

The shadow of Red Walls House suffocated Talia. The vile energy of the place hummed through her, pulsed in the injuries she received inside. The sensations split so intensely over her belly that she had to press her hand to the welted scar to prove to herself she wasn't ripping open and bleeding. In all her panic, she neglected her breathing, and the night wobbled around her.

"This place is terrifying," Ricky said.

"We have never been this close," Willow whispered.

"Who would want to be?" Ricky said.

"Even when we dared each other to ride our bikes up the drive." Willow tipped her head back to look at the roof. "It is huge."

"And full of terrors," Talia mumbled.

"I'm so sorry, Tal."

When Talia turned, Willow was facing her. "For what?"

"That you were in there. That you had to go through all this."

Talia knew that wrinkle in Willow's brow, that purse of her lips. She had seen them every day in the first few months after Juni, then again every anniversary, every fleeting mention or memory.

Talia hated that face.

"It was my fault." Sighing, Talia looked to the high window. "I did this to them."

"Oh no." Ricky whirled on her. "You may have been fucking stupid to get drunk and try to walk home from a party alone. You may be a terrible friend for lying to us." He paused as Willow scowled at him. "But none of this is your fault. The only people to blame are those…" He followed Talia's gaze. "Monsters."

He used her word. Almost like he believed her.

"Let's get in there." Ricky bounced on his feet, then turned to the porch.

Willow snatched his arm with a trembling hand. "We can't just march in the front door. We don't even have weapons!"

"I don't know that weapons would help." Staring into the house's eyes, Talia eased around the building, twigs snapping and cracking under her steps, leaving her friends to follow her.

"I think this might be worse than the story that the Red Walls House's owner murdered his entire family at holiday dinner and buried them in the basement," Willow nearly whispered.

"Even the part about him eating them, too," Ricky added, and they both shuddered.

Talia did not acknowledge them. She remained locked on the structure as she circled it.

"They also say it's a coven of vampires that come out at night," Willow continued. "Tal, do you think that's what they are? Are vampires real now?"

Talia froze, hesitant to turn away from the house. "The truth is worse," she said to the walls in front of her. "Way worse." To her friends. "I don't know what they are. Not vampires. Not cannibals. Something worse." Back to the house.

Her words silenced her friends. They crept to the back of the building. Dim firelight spilled from a window, dancing on the glass fragments on the ground. At their glint, Talia's steps quickened, hurrying to the broken window.

On tip toe, she peered through the frame. Touching the sill, she could almost feel her parents there. She leaned in to chase their echo. The fire burned low in the hearth, casting twisted shadows over the empty furniture. She looked over and over again, examining every corner she could see.

"We can go in this way," she said.

With a curt nod, Ricky knelt to boost Talia through.

"Then what?" Willow curled her arms into her chest and remained at the edge of the shadows.

"We'll figure it out. Lo, come on!" Ricky waved her on, but she shifted her weight from side to side. "Lo!"

Talia clapped her hand over Ricky's mouth, his hot breath pooling in her palm. She flicked her eyes inside as they all waited. When she released Ricky's face, he glowered at Willow. Stabbing his finger into the air at her, then the window, he commanded her to them. She turned to the darkness before crouching beside them.

The three hunched near the ground, exchanging glances. Willow's eyes bulged with fear, while Ricky's narrowed with purpose.

Nodding to them, Talia rose. As she placed her hands in the window frame, Ricky offered his knee, and she crawled inside. Willow followed; then Ricky heaved himself after.

The smell saturated Talia. Her nerves arched at it, lighting up pain points on her body. Nausea doubled her over, and acid raged up her throat.

"Tal? Tal." Willow placed her hand between Talia's shoulders.

The touch shocked her, like a burn on her back. She jerked away, then forced herself back into her friend's comfort.

"Okay. Okay," Willow cooed, guiding Talia to the sprawling red couch. "You're okay. Breathe."

Talia closed her eyes and only saw the red room, only felt the stone table and the pain, only smelled Lamont's musk. Everything hit all at once, and it made her head spin.

Willow's hand rubbed up and down her back, slow and light, barely on the edge of her awareness. Ricky's weight settled beside her. Feeling them around her, she inhaled until the red room faded away.

"They're in the red room." Talia dug her fists into her face, then propped them under her chin.

"What's the red room?" The fight had left Ricky's voice. It flowed smoothly, like when he spoke Spanish. Words pouring over her ears.

"It's where they hurt me." Sniffing, she stood. "They have this altar thing. It's something they do a lot."

"Like a ritual," Ricky said.

Ricky and Willow rose and huddled in close. Talia clutched at both of them, grounding herself in the feeling of their warm flesh against her fingers. She was not alone in the house this time. She was not the victim this time. She had chosen to come in, was here to save her parents.

"I have a plan," she said.

FIFTEEN

AUTUMN WILLED HERSELF not to cry. The rage and the frustration blazed through her face, set her sinuses on fire. Her entire being only wanted to release the molten tears.

She just wanted to hold Talia again.

I should have listened. Her voice berated her inside her head. *I should have stayed in that bathroom, washing her hair and listening to her. I wasn't kind enough. I wasn't understanding enough. I was so blind, so fucking stupid. I hate when he's right.*

Turning to Colin, she found him already looking at her. Gleaming blue irises drowning in dilated pupils. The panic in his eyes resembled his affection if she peeled the surrounding expression away. Both the sight of his terror and the reminder of his love beckoned the tears again.

Fuck. She would not cry.

Lina lingered at the end of the table by Autumn's feet. Her thin, mocking lips moved around words and giggles. Lamont replied as he drifted toward her. They looked drunk on glee. Like a couple excited for a dinner party.

Autumn could no longer hear their words. She had tuned out their jeers until they dissolved into the background. Torturous tones, dancing in the air around her.

Colin shifted beside her, his leg brushing hers. She would have given anything to touch him, to cling to him. She would have given more to hold her daughters. Or at least the one left to save.

Ma, you don't understand. You don't know what they are.

Her daughter was right. She could have never imagined whatever they were. She thought she was diving into vengeance with normal humans. Would she have stayed home if she knew what they would be facing, if she knew she would damn them all? Squeezing her eyes shut, in the pit of her riling stomach, yes, she would have come. No matter what.

Nothing could have kept her from the revenge she'd been denied with Juni.

"They are marinating." Lina's nails running down Autumn's leg brought Autumn back to the room.

"The same flavors?" Lamont leaned over Colin's shoes, sniffing at them.

"Oh yes. Fear." Lina flicked a long nail at Colin. "And anger." Then to Autumn.

"Both make the organs delicious." Lamont smirked. "I wonder what flavor the girl will be this time."

Beside Autumn, Colin yanked on his cord, then whimpered in pain. Autumn rolled toward him but was tethered by her own agony. There were the tears again. Blinking them back, she released an enraged yowl instead.

The monsters just grinned, feasting on their suffering.

A faint crash interrupted their exploitation. The monsters abandoned their languish against the table, snapping tall. Lina glared at the open door, tilting her head to listen. Lamont's eyes remained fixed on Lina to gauge her reaction.

"Glass," she said low. "Our little lamb."

Autumn's heart stopped. Colin went rigid beside her. They held their breath together.

"Go retrieve her, will you?" Lina gently shoved Lamont towards the door.

His lumbering footfalls announced his movement down the hall. Autumn could not breathe; she could not will herself to suck in the breath.

Talia. She wanted to see her again. But not here.

"Family reunion," Lina sang as she rounded the table.

Stopping beside Colin, she lifted a hand. The cracking sound drew Autumn's attention from her fevered thoughts. Lina's fingers snapped and jerked as they grew longer, the harsh point of the nail extending. Her fingers became claws, talons.

What the fuck are they?

"Who wants to go first?" Lina threatened the sharp points over them. "We have already tasted the baby. What about Daddy?" She twisted her wrist toward Colin. "Do you taste as sweet as your daughter?"

The nails drew closer to Colin's face, flirting with his eyelashes. Until the smell crept into the room.

Lifting her nose and turning away from her prey, she sniffed at the air. She stepped toward the door, looking through narrowed eyes. The smell only grew stronger. It seemed to fill the room now.

Glancing back at the table, she stomped out to the hall.

Alone in the room, Autumn and Colin lay stunned for an instant. Keeping their eyes and ears locked on the door, they waited. Only more of that smoky odor.

They turned to each other. As much as they could. Autumn's arms itched to reach out to Colin—to hug him, to free him. Yet she could not take the pain of pulling again. Colin's eyes had shifted from fear to a morbid hope.

"Is that smoke?" he asked, shimmying as close to his wife as he could.

"I think so. Is the house on fire?"

Autumn sighed and looked to the ceiling. She couldn't see the smoke yet, was not coughing. It was just the smell.

"Do you think it's Talia?" Talia's face flashed across her mind as she said it, lowered resigned in the bathtub.

"I hope not," Colin huffed as he continued to struggle within the limits of his bondage.

"What do we do, Colin?" The defeat in her own voice was evident.

"I don't know." He stiffened. "If only we had had a plan coming into this." He paused, bit his lip. "I'm sorry, Autumn. I didn't mean that."

Autumn felt the impact of his words in her chest. Closing her eyes, she hid in the dark, sucking in her lips.

"Yes, you did," she mumbled.

She hated when he was right.

From behind her eyelids, she heard steps approaching. They seemed lighter than the monster parade, but she cowered anyway. The sharp nails were coming. Those pointy tongues were coming.

"Mom! Dad!" Talia's hushed voice overflowed with relief.

Autumn could have levitated off the table at the sight of her child, the braids she placed still in her hair.

"Talia," Colin was saying. "Talia, baby, you have to get out of here. They're waiting for you. They're looking for you."

"Baby, go home." Autumn nearly choked on the words. Talia was so close she could feel her energy, her presence. "Just go to Ricky's or Willow's. Get some help."

"They're with me." Talia grasped the rope wound through her father.

"What?" Autumn raised her head from the slab.

"Ricky and Willow. They're here. Making a distraction."

"No no no no no, baby." Colin lifted his head. "You have to go. You all have to go."

Talia moved around the table, hunting the perimeter of objects and offerings until she found a knife. "We're not going anywhere. We have to handle this."

Autumn winced as she heard her own foolish words spilling from her daughter.

SIXTEEN

RICKY MET WILLOW under the stairs, as Talia had instructed. Willow's hair tumbled from her bun and hung in strings around her splotchy, pink face. Ricky gathered her close and pressed them into the dark.

Lamont came first, lumbering down the stairs. Dust rained down, as if the steps were ready to collapse and reveal them. Ricky snuck a hand over Willow's mouth to hush her fearful gasps.

They waited, barely breathing, hugging each other.

Lina's steps were not as heavy but forceful, confident. She dropped from the stairs with long strides, blowing past Ricky and Willow as she chased the smoke to the sitting room, where all their visitors had entered.

"Set a little fire to distract us," Lamont said from the room.

"I do appreciate her spirit," Lina chuckled.

The voices did not sound like monsters. Ricky did not know what he was expecting. He strained to hear, struggled to let his imagination paint them. He held Willow for another breath, staring at the shadows down the hall. Then, gripping her hand, he led her from under the stairs. They crept around and up the staircase, testing and failing to avoid creaks. The pace was excruciating, but eventually, they summited the rickety flight.

Red room. Red room. Talia had said to meet them in a red room. What had she meant red room? In the dark hallway of closed doors, nothing looked red. Willow's hand trembled in his. He took a step forward then back, casting eyes left and right, unsure. How many doors were in this hallway?

He waited too long. From the bottom of the stairs, they heard Lamont's stomps approaching. There was no more thinking. No more finding the red room. Ricky dove around the corner and down the hall, snatching a door and yanking Willow after him. He closed them in as soft as he could.

Lamont did not ascend the stairs, but they could hear his and Lina's voices bantering in increasing tones. Ricky could not tell if they were arguing or laughing. He crouched beside the door, listening.

Willow turned away and swept the room. Her eyes settled on the gaping maw of a bear in the corner. Startling, she leaped back into Ricky.

"What is this?" Ricky stepped away from the door and toward the long table, his fingers hovering and wandering over the artifacts.

"It's a fucking bear." Willow brought her arms around herself.

Ricky leaned in toward the shields, squinting at the pawns and small figures. "All these swirly knot designs. Your parents have this shit, right? Don't you know what this is?"

"I'm Irish. Mostly, I think. Not whatever this is." She waved her hand around, like an accusation at the room.

"We have to find Talia."

Willow's eyes widened and her clutch tightened.

"She said red room." Ricky looked around the room. "Not red."

Quivering, Willow stared at him.

"They're still downstairs. You want to wait for them here?" Ricky offered his hand.

"I'm sorry, Daddy." Talia winced as she rubbed the knife blade along the cord. Colin chomped at his bottom lip, his face and scalp going redder with every movement. "It's tied too tight down there. I'm sorry. I'm sorry."

She sawed until the cord snapped. Releasing a bundled breath, Colin lowered his arms, drawing them in as he sat up. Then she looked to her mother. Autumn offered a calm gaze, but her eyes were smoldering. As Talia cut the cord, Autumn tensed and held her breath, but she did not move. She just kept regarding her daughter with an odd, yet familiar, stare.

Like beside the bathtub.

Sitting up beside Colin, Autumn cradled her hand. She tugged on the cord, grimacing and recoiling, her fingers jerking. Talia watched her steel herself, going rigid on the stone, before she unthreaded the cord in one long movement. Blood splattered from the open wound. Colin turned agape and looked down at his hand.

"You don't have to do it." Autumn almost laughed, blood pooling in her palms.

Eyes narrowed and head reddening, Colin freed himself from the bind.

Both of her parents were bleeding on the floor. There was nothing to stop it, and Talia was sure the monsters downstairs could smell it.

The dinner bell.

She braced her mother then father off the table. They skidded from the edge and crumpled on the floorboards. They looked so small, so wounded, huddled together at the end of the table, cradling their bleeding wounds.

The way they looked when Colin put his arm around Autumn at Juni's burial. Sun blazing down, brighter than it had any right to over such an event.

Talia's mind flickered between the moments, the two strobing into one horrible picture. The hole in her chest opened like that hole in the dirt. For an instant, she forgot about surviving.

"What now?" Autumn asked.

Talia paced in front of the door, tugging at the ends of her braids. She felt the weight of all their lives stacked on her shoulders, piled on her chain of awful decisions.

"We have to get out of here." Colin pushed up from the table.

What are we going to do? The question pulsated in Talia's head, growing louder with each passing second. *Where are Ricky and Willow? What the fuck are we going to do? I got them into this. Now we're all going to die. Because of me.*

"What about this window?" Colin stumbled over, pressing his face to the glass and looking to the ground below. "It's not that far of a drop. We would probably be okay, better than in here."

Autumn eased beside him, peering down. She nodded, and he shoved at the pane. The window did not budge. He fumbled at the locks, ran his wounded, bloody fingers over all the seams. When he yanked again, it remained unmoved.

"We could break it," he said. "We—"

A low scratching interrupted him. The noise climbed the stairs, the sound of long and unnatural nails carving into the wall. It dragged along Talia's brain and ignited the scar along her belly. The nails were back in her skin. They were coming.

"I smell you, little lamb," Lina's voice sang from under the door. "Or do I smell the bleeding sheep?"

Talia could hear Lina's fiendish smile in the words. She looked between her parents, the bleeding sheep clutching their wounded hands.

"Go!" Talia hissed. "We have to go! We're standing where they feed."

Yanking the door open, Talia shoved at her father, desperate and shooing out her mother. None of them had any idea where to go. They bunched together outside the door, groping at each other and flailing in shadows that made the hallway seem cavernous. Full of uncertainty and dire possibilities.

Talia turned toward the steps, dim light climbing from the first floor.

"Sometimes, I do like to play with my food," Lina laughed. Closer now.

In a panic, Talia rushed them past the steps, anywhere away from the sinister voice. There was only one other way. Down in the shadows. The family moved as one fearful mass. She could feel all their heartbeats slamming against each other in the humid mix of ragged exhales.

Then the footsteps became hefty. Lamont.

The monsters were near now. They had to be upstairs, right at the end of the dark hallway, right outside the red room.

In the dark, past the stairs, they stuttered to a stop. Through the weak light, Talia could make out the doors to two rooms. Ominous black rectangles in the wall. A narrower closet door sat in between. Her parents stopped before the far door, Talia ended up right in front of the gaping closet. It looked deep and dark enough to consume her.

Lamont's footfalls crashed toward them, Lina's vile snickers chasing behind. The floor vibrated, sounds crowded the hall, forcing the group to cower away. Her parents were too far away; the monsters were too close. On instinct, the prey scattered.

"Hide!" Talia shouted as she dove into the closet and kicked the door shut behind her.

"Talia, no!" Autumn shouted on the other side of the door. She heard the far door and hoped her parents were tucked out of sight behind it.

Dust crusted along Talia's fingers as she drew her hands over the floorboards. The old and neglected smell packed her nostrils. Yet she could hear everything, echoing like an amphitheater in the closed walls. Even her own breathing roared around her.

"Little lamb."

Lina's voice licked along her ear, a whisper with thin and pointed tongue. Talia ducked back against the darkness, knocking into the back of the closet.

Then it was gone. The wall, the closet. Talia hung in a shapeless abyss. The world above and below her receded, and she was only the gap between. That suspended second ticked by, and she plunged into that darkness. Her scream followed her down.

She careened down steep and slick metal, hands floundering and clawing at the rough wood. Her shattering shriek dwindled to confused grunts. The floor greeted her to knock the air out of her chest and leave her as a deflated pile on the packed dirt.

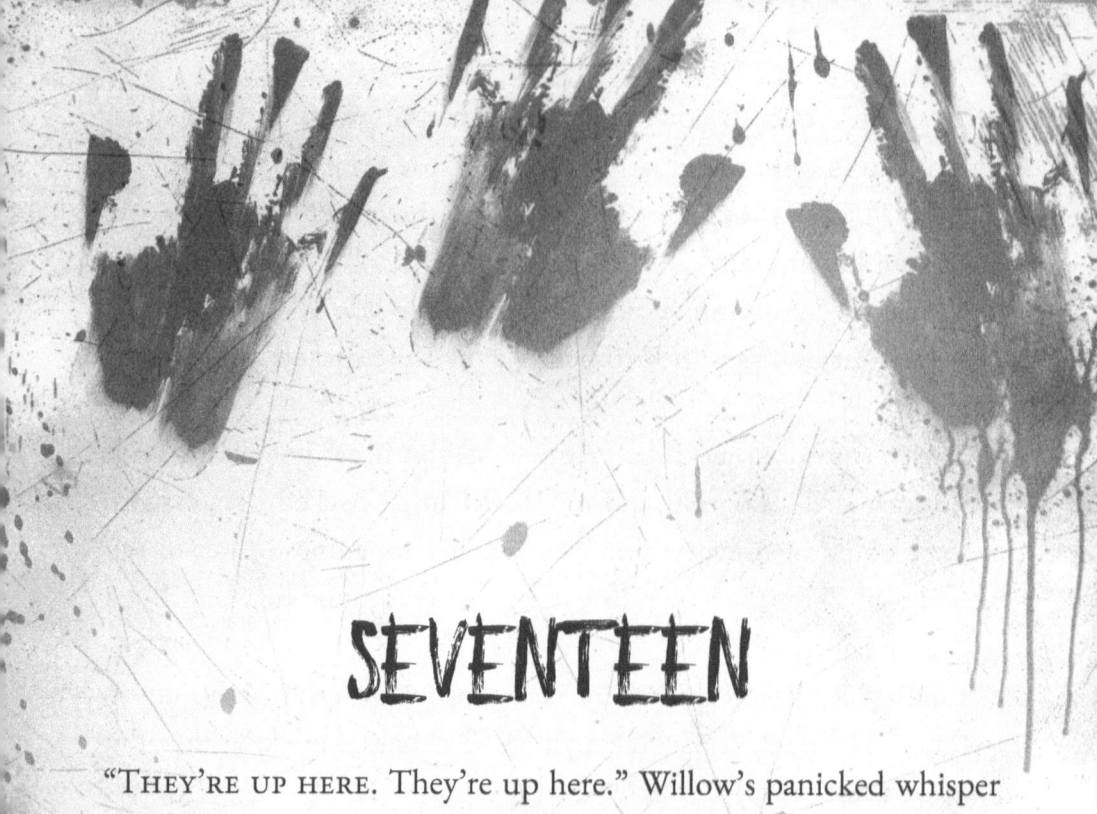

SEVENTEEN

"THEY'RE UP HERE. They're up here." Willow's panicked whisper chased Ricky through the dark.

Her convulsing hand kept trying to tremble out of his grip, but he held her like a vice, dragging her along the hallway wall. As he listened for the monster steps, he came back around the corner, and his hand groped until he found the next room. He seized the doorknob like a lifeline and dove through the threshold.

He stumbled through the door as Willow shut and barred it with her petite body. A standing lamp in the corner blinded him and illuminated a fresh museum of horrors.

Still not a red room. But a room full of red.

"What the fuck is this?" he breathed.

Willow answered him with a gaping mouth and matching eyes.

Beside the lamp, long, wide shelves climbed the wall. A massive chest of drawers lined the other wall. Ricky shrank away. Nowhere to go in the tight room. Nowhere but a hallway full of monsters. Each shelf lined with clear jars filled with clear liquid. And flesh. A heap of eyes looking back at him. Large red beans of kidneys. Slabs of livers. Balloons of lungs. Broken hearts. Separated, categorized, preserved.

Ricky gagged, strangling the urge with a hand over his mouth as Willow flushed green beside him.

"How many sets of eyes are those?" she breathed.

"I don't even know if there are any sets." Ricky surveilled the browns, blues, greens, hazels, watching them from behind the glass.

"How long have they been doing this?" Willow teared up. "How many people?"

The carnage distracted them. Entombed in the macabre, they forgot they were in flight. They froze in the shadow of so much gore until they heard the scratching nails reach the door. The fingers raked over the wall, sinking claws in their fear. Ricky recoiled from the door, striking the chest. He flinched away from the rattling jars. Willow reached over for his hand, and he clutched it back.

As they held each other and shook against the slaughter behind them, the nails drummed a sharp and terrible rhythm on the door. Their song beckoned Ricky and Willow's terror, drawing it to a painful crescendo.

"Oh my god," Willow whispered against Ricky's neck. "Oh my god. Oh my god."

Her voice burrowed into his brain. The alarm in her words tugged something up from deep at his center. Something heavy that smothered the fear with purpose. Pushing up from the chest, he guided her behind him.

He could protect her. This could be his moment. He could prove he was better right here. Better than the forecast in his father's shadow. Without the volunteering and the clubs and the grades and the advocacy. No waiting until he fucked it up or substances found him in college. The thought was stupid. Even in the moment, he knew the logic was broken, pathological. Yet with the threat scratching the door, his step forward just happened.

The tapping stopped. A silence swelled in its place. It expanded long enough for Ricky and Willow to lower their shoulders and turn to each other.

As soon as they exhaled, the door careened into the room, colliding with the wall, leaving Lina framed by its void. She leaned her arm into the door jamb and resumed clicking her nails against the wood. The nails grew long, making her hand resemble a pale and spindly spider. Her wide, white eyes turned pinpoints of black pupils to ingest her prey's terror.

She tipped her head back as her tongue stretched long and gray. It waved over her mouth like a flag.

"Oh, fuck," Ricky exclaimed. His face twisted in confusion. Nothing else he could say. Yet he remained fixed in front of Willow.

Lina slurped her tongue into grinning jaws and leveled her blanched eyes back on them. She hesitated and savored every step toward them. Willow squeezed Ricky's hand, reminding him that she was there, that he was not facing this monster alone in terrifying solitude, that there was more beside him than preserved organs. That he had purpose, that he could do something right.

Pressing Willow back, Ricky stepped ahead of her, one step closer to the monster. His thoughts blazed in his ears but did not form words, like all the cries he wanted to release but kept bundled in his chest. Inflating by each excruciating second.

Lina pressed a hand to her chest, her nails reaching past her shoulder. "Love tenderizes the meat. Bravery makes it sweet. All those endorphins still crackling in the flesh. Like the dying on the battlefield. One foot into Valhalla and the other marinating in sweet suffering."

Willow's hand curled into the back of Ricky's shirt. Her grip shook as much as her breaths on his neck. The fear in her touch put his teeth on edge. He wished he was bigger, stronger, braver. Better.

Lina lifted a finger to her lips and wound her tongue around it. Then she lunged forward. Impossible speed, closing the space between them in a breath.

The nails sank into Ricky, digging in deep beneath his collarbones. His purpose shattered into a mosaic of pain. Wailing, he grabbed at Lina's wrists in an attempt to push her out of him. The flaming licks of pain blanked his mind, made him only the struggle.

"Your fear will taste so good," she cooed in his ear. "And something else." She sniffed him. "Mmmmmm."

Heaving him up by his wounds, she pitched him into the shelves. His back collided with the top shelf, shattering the jars and bathing him in their dissected, preserved contents. The shards bit into his skin as he plummeted through the other shelves to accumulate their awful mixtures. He smashed into the chest, then flopped at Willow's feet, saturated and bleeding.

The puddle of failure he always feared he would be.

"Ricky!" Willow shrieked, reaching for him.

The pain throbbed over Ricky in a distant hum, sensations lost beneath his fury, fear, and disappointment, the adrenaline coursing through him. Like a numb limb coming back to the nerves. Glass chomped into him with every movement as he struggled to crawl and extend a hand to Willow.

Willow's fingers flirted with his, then were yanked away. He groped at vacant air.

Her cries split the world. They blasted into Ricky's ears and flowed under his skin. The most pained and terrified he had ever heard. More unnerving than when his mother was giving birth in the next room of their impossibly small house. To any of his four siblings. More desperate than his father's wails through detox.

Dragging himself over the crunching floor, flowing over a spiked river of organs and meat, he scrambled as much as his damaged body would allow him. Lina clutched Willow by the throat. Her squirming tongue carved singes into Willow's contorted face.

Ricky had never seen her so red, face ablaze enough to make her hair look dim. And it was his fault. The monster should be taking him.

Maybe she still would. When she was done.

Lina raked her claws over Willow's shoulder, the lines swelling in blood through her shirt. Willow's outcry nearly deafened the room. Wrath and tears poured down Ricky's face. He managed to grapple his bloody hand around Lina's ankle and squeezed with all his shaking strength.

Lina laughed and rolled white eyes down to him. "I'm not ready for the second course yet."

Keeping Willow's throat cinched in her hand, she punted Ricky back to the glassy puddle, his ribs cracking at the impact. He coughed as he wrapped a hand around the new, louder pain.

"Willow," he rasped, mashing his forearms into the carnage.

Turning to him, Lina opened her horrible mouth wide, exposing a second row of razored teeth, and gave him a wink. She plunged a nail into Willow's abdomen, where her sternum ended. Willow stopped screaming and rounded around the puncture. Lina ran her tongue over Willow's nose, then ripped the nail down.

Willow split open.

Ricky sputtered and sobbed. Disbelief and horror competed in his mind. What he was seeing could not be possible. That could not be his girl spilling on the floor.

Wincing and whimpering, he drew to his knees, the glass stabbing into untouched flesh. Lina laughed as she reached into Willow and spilled her intestines to the floor. As the meat splattered to the ground and Willow's eyes grew distant, Ricky recoiled and pressed into the chest of drawers. He wished he could tuck himself and his inadequacy into the safety of one of the drawers.

If there was anywhere in this house that could be safe. If he wanted to survive to the other side of this moment.

Burying his face into his arm, he wailed as the snapping and squishing sounds washed over him. He shook his head against it. Lina's feast was between him and the door. And he was next.

The cracking stopped with a sick pop. Then Willow's weight hit the floorboards. Ricky hazarded a glance. Lina stood in the blood puddle, arching her back and lifting the fist-sized organ above her face. Her tongue teased at the edge of Willow's heart. She froze and jerked her head to Ricky, smirk twisting her bloody lips.

She tossed the heart like lobbing a ball. It smacked into Ricky's chest, leaving a bloody print on his shirt, then flopped to the floor beside him between a few eyeballs and a deflated lung.

Ricky stopped breathing. Nausea and panic, and the anticipation of death, skittered over him in twitching waves, fast enough to inhibit thoughts.

He only knew he had lost Willow, and he was next.

He braced for it, waited for Lina to march over the smashed jars and send her claws through all the sweet parts of him. Instead, her sadistic cackle drew away from him. He looked up to watch her seize Willow's ankle and drag the limp body from the room.

EIGHTEEN

COLIN STILL HAD his arms wrapped around Autumn after dragging her through the door. He held her back, held her close. For a stunned second, they stared at the door, listening to the muffled movement and screams.

That was Talia was all Autumn could think. *I killed my baby.*

"What did you do?" Whirling, she slapped at his chest. Something died inside her, causing her body to slacken in her husband's embrace. "What did you do?"

His mouth gaped for a moment before finding the words. "She told us to hide. She dove into that door. I—"

"You left her!" Despite the room closing in around her, her mind flipped between braiding Talia's hair in the bathroom and holding her tight after ballet class. The regret, the guilt that had wound its way around her skeleton and through her capillaries since she lost Juni blossomed, opening horrible, poisonous blooms.

"No. They can chase us instead. They can eat us instead of her," he insisted.

"We have to go back for them," she whispered. "We left her. They're kids, Colin. We left them."

They should have been standing between them and the monsters, not hunching in the shadows of this bizarre chamber.

Without waiting for his reply, she dove for the doorknob. The cold of the metal zinged on her nerves. She wrenched hard, yet it remained fixed. She jiggled again and again, careless of the noise, but it did not budge.

He reached forward to still her. The warmth of the embrace made her hesitate before she glared up at him and moved away. He caught her arms before she went for the door again.

"We have to get to her," she shouted.

"Shhhh! We can't just break down the door. She won't stay hidden if we lead him to her."

Was she hidden now? Autumn hadn't seen where Talia darted. Was she with Ricky and Willow?

She hated when he was right. She had made it worse. Her instincts were strong yet blind. Every part of her flexed and begged to find her child, put eyes on her, hold her tight. Her emotions boiled inside her chest, frothing and overflowing to fill her skull. She felt agitated in her skin. Nowhere to go, nothing to do. Nothing existed but that door she could not breach.

She took a step back and finally looked over the room in the faint light of small lamps with false flames. Not candles like around the altar but lightbulbs fashioned to imitate fire. A massive bed hung suspended from thick chains. Wispy black fabric twirled around and between the chains. Slick satin sheets spilled over the mattress and pillows. Below it, a smaller bed hid in its shadow. The bedding heaped on it as if the occupant had just roused. The blanket appeared to be made of fur.

Sharp and angled symbols covered the walls. Carved, painted, and drawn over the room, forming a constellation of characters. The foreign shapes reflected in their eyes. She had no idea what they meant, but she knew it was something awful.

Then the door shuddered in its frame. With each monstrous footstep on the other side, it quaked on its hinges.

"He's coming." Colin drew her back from the door.

"We're trapped in here," she said.

We'll never get to her. He's going to burst in and corner us, she thought. *Then feast on our organs. Then finish Talia.*

Yet she silently hoped he would come for them, forgetting all about her daughter.

Colin released her and scrambled behind her. She squinted after him. Uncharacteristically frantic, he traced the wall, pushing at the windows. His normally methodical movements trembled at the edges, curled with desperation.

"These don't open. We could smash one." He spun to find an object to throw.

"And that's better than breaking down the door, how?" Touching her fingers to her forehead, she clutched herself. She was pretty sure the monsters already knew where they were. Of course they were trapped in here. This didn't feel like hunting; it felt like a game.

Lamont's steps marched toward them, making the hallway seem endless. Autumn almost wished for his arrival to end the barbed suspense. For any way out of this room.

But she had wished for her own end so many times in the past decade.

"Then what do you suggest we do?" Colin's voice lowered, his brow twisting.

There were no thoughts, no plans after *get to Talia*. Just as there had been nothing after *hurt them back*. Now, there was just acidic remorse climbing her throat. In the shapeless pain, she felt she was going to accomplish neither.

All her fault. Just like Juni.

The boots stopped and scraped outside the door. Why was he stopping? Why was he taking his time? For all their frenzy, the monster chasing them plodded along like a slasher.

Yet dread at his proximity reignited their cause. Shoving the curtains aside, Colin pawed for something to chuck through the glass. He found his way to the long, dark bookcases consuming the far wall. Their shelves sagged under so many dusty and warped tomes. Each looking ancient and foreign.

Landing on a thick bookend, he snatched it up and heaved it at the window. With a dull smack, the bookend collided with the window, then tumbled down the curtain to the floorboards. The glass did not break or even crack.

He dove for the bookend. Clutching it tight, he bashed it into the glass again and again. The window did not even sound like glass, the impact thicker, unaffected. After six strikes, he lowered his arm and let the object tumble from his fingers.

He stared after it, slumped in defeat, then returned to the shelves.

Autumn shrank beside him, eyes fixed on the door. Lamont was still right outside. She could nearly hear his hot breath on the wood. A dark part of her willed him to come in and get it over with. If his hands were around her throat, they could not be around Talia's. She could settle for being a successful diversion.

When she bumped into Colin, he stopped searching. His shoulders fell as he turned to cradle her. She savored his touch, the pleasant feeling of him before the pain came. She could take this breath before they took this turn. They clung to each other until the door creaked open. Lamont's heavy frame cut a menacing shadow. He gave them a smoldering grin.

Tangled in each other, they lurched back, pressing into the bookshelf. With a deep click and whir, the bookshelf jerked before spinning them out of the room.

From the other side, they heard Lamont's loud, sadistic chuckle.

NINETEEN

The basement came into focus slowly for Talia. Her skull pounded loud enough to ring her ears. Peeling her eyes open, she lifted her throbbing head. Her entire body objected. It begged to remain flattened on the dirt floor, wrapped up in the dank smell around her.

For an instant, she forgot where she was. Her brain told her she was waking up on Monere Lane, unearthing herself from her intoxication to stumble alone on the street. Then that fantasy bled into Lina's voice.

Little lamb.

With a gasp, Talia jerked upright, coughing and wilting over her own knees. In her aching huddle, she scanned the room around her.

The basement was dug deep enough for the ceiling to loom high above her. Yet it offered no windows. Her pupils worked with the light tumbling down from the shaft. She evaluated her entryway to the room. The square gaped over her, the metal slide she slid down extending out like a tongue. She could make out shelves and piles along the walls around her.

And the shape of a cellar door.

Then sounds snatched her attention. Far above, with the light, there came faint yelling and screaming. Concentrating hard, she stretched her hearing to its limit.

Ricky and Willow.

Her heart broke at the anguish in those sounds. Sounds she had never heard her friends make. The sob racked her wounded frame. She grabbed her cheeks and stared up the shaft. Their pain deafened her as they seemed impossibly out of reach.

Then Lamont's laugh, distant but loud, startled her. What could he possibly be laughing at? Her stomach turned.

She focused hard and heard him start to move. His steps were muted so far away, yet they still announced his movements. They marched past the opening to the shaft, receded across the ceiling, hesitated, then moved back. She tracked the sound with her eyes. They returned right above her and stopped. For an instant, the light above was eclipsed.

"Fuck," she breathed.

He knew she was down here. Or if he hadn't found her parents, he knew someone was down here.

Her parents. *Are they still alive? Did I get them killed?*

She did not have time for thoughts. She would have to find out for herself.

Lamont's approach came in steady percussion. Someone beating a funeral march on a bass drum. Down the hall, hammering the stairs. Talia didn't know how the house had survived the weight and aggression of him.

Her body tucked its pain below her purpose. As she dragged herself to her feet, her head spun, and the room swam for a moment. She rocked on her legs before steadying. She limped to the shelves and let her fingers dance in search of a weapon. Something, anything to give her a few moments, incapacitate him so she could run and get upstairs, get her out of this dead-end room.

Lamont stopped. The hinges of the door whined as he opened it. Light spilled down, painting a staircase she had not even seen.

"I can smell you from here," he called.

Talia groped over the shelves as he loomed at the top of the stairs. With more light, she could see more of the contents, yet it did not help. They were all haphazardly heaped or scattered across the wood. Dusty glass bottles, wooden hammers, folded chains. She flinched away from the unexpected softness of a pile of gloves.

As Lamont started his descent, she seized something heavy and metal. It scratched the shelf as she extracted it. A thick metal bar. A crowbar maybe? She didn't care. It had enough heft to cause damage.

To a human, at least.

She receded slow, as slow as Lamont moved down each step. He was teasing her, toying with her just like Lina.

His master? Talia mused in her withdrawal. *His maker?* Lina's voice echoed in her mind. *Anger... Fear... They're marinating.*

He was making her taste better. The realization squeezed her stomach, and she gagged.

"You tasted so sweet last time." Lamont's voice crept into her ears. "I never thought I would get to lick your blood again. I bet you only taste better knowing all your people will die in this place. Hopelessness and regret are such flavors."

Talia winced at the mention of her people. A frantic slideshow of all the ways they could be tortured flickered in front of her. The red light, that massive stone table, threaded restraints, sharp nails, cauterizing tongues. She shook her head hard to return to the moment. Taking measured steps, as if she could hide if she was slow and silent, she backed into the wall.

Not the wall, the cellar doors.

Glaring to the stairs, she saw Lamont's boots drop into view. She kept the bar in her grip but turned her attention to the doors. She shook the wood to hear it rattle. It was old and brittle against her hands. She ignored the promise of splinters.

Two more steps closer. He couldn't see her yet.

She glimpsed the two holes bored into the door, where the chain would run to lock it shut. The fading night poured in through the openings. No chain. These monsters did not need to lock anything. The name of Red Walls House was enough to deter even the boldest citizen. No one wanted to be in this basement.

Bracing against the dirt, Talia shoved at the doors. They were heavier than she anticipated. Or blocked from the outside. She pushed again and again. There were not many steps left on the staircase. He would see her at any moment.

Conjuring Ricky and Willow's distant cries in her ears, she threw herself into the doors. They hopped at her effort. Fumbling her feet under her, she held the gap open, gaining leverage on the door, widening the rift to worm her hand through. Then she shouldered the door and tripped up the low steps.

Lamont landed on the dirt floor as she breached the cellar door. He released a confused and angry sound, then leaned into a heavy run. Talia scrambled from the opening, still clutching the door. Once she felt dead grass beneath her shoes, she heaved the door closed behind her. It banged down on its wooden frame. She looked at the gaping holes under metal handles. No latch, no lock. Her body would not be enough.

Then she remembered the bar in her hand. She threaded it through the handles and took a step back. Lamont hit it in a flurry of foreign shouts and rattling hinges. It would not hold him for long, but it was the moment she needed. She spun and hurried away from the cellar.

Dropping into a basketball sprint, she rushed around the house, headed for the awful front door. The face of the house still glared down at her, winking its red eye with all the horrors behind that window.

In the rising dawn, she glanced around. The forest looked different in the faint orange light, shapes and trees lifting out of the night. Through their dead branches, she could make out the curl of Monere Lane. The fumbling path she took through the trees to spill back on that asphalt. The way she had escaped this house a few hours ago.

It felt like a lifetime ago, like a past life.

The escape route beckoned to her. A second freedom lay at her feet. If they all were dead already, she could steal herself away to her grief.

Did she even want to survive this?

More screams floated from the house. Ricky yelled Willow's name. The path vanished from Talia's mind, and she ran back up to Red Walls House.

She burst through the front door, unlocked like the cellar. She had the flitting realization that she could have rushed past her own fingernail marks on the frame. She ran through an icy wave of her own fear, the echo of her entrance to this place. Tempering her sprints, she reached the bottom of the stairs and gripped the banister.

She focused on the sounds coming from upstairs. The pierce of Ricky's cry muffled into distant banter, sounds without the shapes of words. Lina's laugh rained down, playing with her food.

Who is she eating? Talia could barely ask herself. *Who is she killing?*

Was it merely a buffet of everyone she loved?

She had to know. She had to do something. Vile curiosity surged through her. She had to force herself to slow. She was moving too fast; she could not move fast enough.

Scratching and struggle mixed with whimpers. Each sound set her teeth on edge, exploded her mind in traumatic possibilities as she drew closer. Who was Lina eating? Who was still alive?

"I'm not ready for the second course yet," Lina's voice rang clear, as if she were right beside Talia.

Another thump and crash brought more crying. Talia's mind whirled, trying to decide who was making the sound, who the first course was. She could not settle on a scenario that would not eviscerate her.

A rip and heavy splat initiated a melody of sobs punctuated by Lina's laughter. Talia froze on the steps. When she heard the dragging, she flattened down on them, letting them bite at her chest and belly. She lowered her eyes level with the floor, giving herself an ant's perspective.

Lina sauntered into view, consuming the hallway and flashing a bloody grin. Talia squinted to see what was clutched in her hand. When she did identify it, she caught a gasp in her palm.

The bottom of a shoe. Pale pink Converse, Talia knew them well. A limp foot.

She did not want to know. She had to. She wanted to throw herself at Lina. She wanted to run away. She remained fixed in the contradictions.

Lina turned sharply into the hall, and Talia smashed herself lower on the stairs. Lina took no notice, basking in the meal at her feet. She moved into the red room and whipped her victim behind her. The baggy gray shirt bunched up to reveal pale flesh. One smooth side of skin before the massive wound opened the body.

The corpse floated on the trail of its own blood that continued to spill from the gaping hole splitting it in half. Talia gagged on her view of an organ peeking from Willow's chest cavity. Willow's head slid past, eyes frozen in resigned horror. Dead yet staring right into Talia. Her curled, bloody fingers were the last thing Talia saw before Willow disappeared into the red room with Lina.

A man reached into the shattered window and pulled out her sister. The limp thing they held so carefully did not look like Juni. As they lowered the unfamiliar body to the ground, Talia watched her bloody, little hand unfurl onto the asphalt, fingers curled into the palm.

Talia tried to cry quietly.

Willow is dead. And with that thought, she saw Willow beside her that long ago night, pink tights and fiery bun, the crooked baby teeth in her smile.

"Lamont." Lina's voice cut her, bringing her back to the dirty stairs in her face.

On cue, heavy sounds shifted below her—Lamont in the basement where she had left him.

"Lamont," Lina called again.

Lamont moved closer, up the basement stairs. The entire house trembled in his wake. Talia forced herself to her feet and down the stairs as quiet as possible. When she hit the floor, Lamont barreled out of the basement door. She darted into the dining room beside the foot of the staircase and pressed to the wall.

Waiting for him to find her. Waiting for him to drag her back to that red room.

But he continued steadily to heed Lina's call.

"You started without me," he said when he reached the room. "Left me chasing that little lamb."

"But I would never finish without you," she answered. "The lamb is not going anywhere." Her wicked giggles drifted down to Talia.

Then the sound became more primal, dissolved into the blend of euphoric babbles and gnawing consumption.

Perhaps Willow was the last course, and Talia was dessert.

She allowed herself to cry, curling into herself to keep it quiet. Tears for Willow. Then she had to find out what happened to the rest of them.

TWENTY

COLIN'S BREATHING TICKLED Autumn's cheek. His arms remained around her, bandaged hand trembling. When he released her, they stepped apart, leaving a hand on each other's arms. It was dark, but it was quiet, and they were alive.

She kept his shirt in her fingers, a marker in the darkness, as she turned in the black. Her grip was weak in her injury. She reached out in front with her undamaged hand, flailed at the blindness. Nothing but thick air until her hand stumbled into a wall. Releasing him, she brought her other hand out in the opposite direction. Another wall. They were in a narrow passage. She could taste the dust in the air. A secret passage?

What kind of Scooby Doo shit is this? she thought.

"Where the fuck are we?" Her voice barely reached a whisper.

He fumbled behind her until he found the walls. "A secret passageway."

In another time, in another place, he would have been so amused to be standing here, yet she noted the tension in his tone. So foreign in his voice.

"He has to know this is here." She looked over her shoulder at where her husband's face hid in the dark. "He has to know we're here."

Hands crawling along the walls, accumulating dust and spiderwebs on her fingertips, she hazarded forward. He kept the back of her shirt in his fist and crept along behind her. With the latest wave of hysteria settling behind them, Autumn returned to her singular motivation.

Talia. Talia was still in this house.

Vengeance had fled from her mind, replaced by the overwhelming focus on survival. Talia's, above all else. In the face of peril, her fear insisted that she find a way to live, yet in this quiet dark, she resigned herself that she might have to pay the penance for her hot-headed fixation.

They slunk down the passage in miniature, shuffled steps. She had no gauge on the time or distance. Seconds hammered in her pulse in her ears. The darkness felt like miles. Were they still behind the bookcases? They had not turned, so they must be along the same face of the house. How big was the house? What else had been in that hall? Another room? A closet? Talia? She had seen it all through frantic panic before they dove into that chamber. It was only shadowed strobes in her mind.

A muffled crash vibrated through the small space. Something from the other side she could feel through her fingertips against the wall. She could not tell where it was coming from, just in front of them somewhere, just out there somewhere. The house seemed impossibly expansive in the dark. Shattering glass edged the impact. Then another collision shook through the wall beneath her hand.

"Ricky!" Willow's shriek pierced their dark solitude.

Colin's hand wrapped tighter in Autumn's shirt. He pressed forward until his chest touched her back. "The kids." His voice climbed above a hush.

The kids they had left.

"But where?" Talia had said Ricky and Willow were here, but Autumn had no idea where. She was already hurrying, hands tiptoeing along the walls as they ping-ponged through the black.

Stifled voices became louder as they hurried down the passage. Even without words, Autumn could identify the tones. Lina's mocking song and Ricky's sobs. But where was Willow? Her voice had dropped out of the concert.

Autumn skidded to a stop, Colin softly running into her. The crunching glass, Ricky's weak cries were right there, as if she could bend down and find him huddled at her feet. Placing her palms to the wall, she winced at the pain shooting up from her hand and listened. Something wet and heavy hit the floor, and Ricky said something low and in anguish.

Willow's name. Without the articulation of the word, Autumn knew.

Then Lina's laugh and an awful dragging sound.

Colin closed his uninjured hand around Autumn's. Both of them leaned into the wall. She let her eyes fall shut, even though it made no difference, and hung her head. She waited, listening to Ricky cry. The sound tugged on everything maternal in her. She wanted to hold him. She needed to hold him. The need resonated in the flesh of her arms, cells singing in the purpose.

It was her fault they were here, too. It was her fault their mothers would know her pain.

She could only imagine what had happened to Willow. Talia's best friend. Tiny legs doing synchronized pliés. The tears were coming, and in these shadows, no one would see.

Colin ran his good hand up and down her back. He knew she was crying, the way he always did.

The lull stretched out long enough for their hearts to find softer patterns. In that space, Autumn animated to search the passage. Pressing, poking, scratching, she frisked for an opening, a seated door, a lever. Whatever had happened at the bookcase. Hearing her, Colin joined her hunt. With his nose against the wall, he traced along it, mapping all its useless imperfections.

They fumbled at the wood until they bumped into each other. He shifted his foot beside her shoes, and a small panel clicked under her feet. Before they could recoil, the wall in front of them scraped along the floor as it rolled ajar. They flinched away from the light as their eyes adjusted.

"Ricky," Autumn breathed as she leaned into the room.

Ricky lay in a bleeding heap on the wet floor, his body racked by sobs. Glass and carnage surrounded him. His face contorted, making him unrecognizable. A red trail curled from the center of the room and out into the hallway.

Willow.

Scrutinizing the room in a rapid glance, checking the corners and any place a monster could hide, Autumn breached the threshold. Glass popped beneath her shoes, and Colin's footsteps crunched behind her. She took two ginger steps in, listening past Ricky for any threatening sound, then hurried over the mess to him.

"Ricky, Ricky baby." She crouched and put her hands on his back and shoulder. "Come here, baby."

Ricky turned his face up to her, eyes swimming in tears. "She took her." He glanced at the heart sitting in a small puddle of blood beside him. "She—she—she…"

Autumn drew him into her chest, smoothing her hands over his wet hair, swiping the tears from his cheeks. His blood saturated the makeshift bandage on her hand. He shuddered at first, then melted in her arms. Wrapping his arm around hers, he clung to her.

The embrace broke her heart.

Colin squatted down, putting a hand of each of them. "Is Willow—" He could not finish.

"I couldn't protect her," Ricky wailed. "I tried. I—" His words surrendered to a sob. "I failed her. I—"

Autumn hushed him against her. It was her failure, not his. Her careless rage had gotten Willow killed. His guilt twisted the knot in her throat tighter. A blend of sorrow and rage coursed through her, burned through her face. Colin gathered them both up, tugging them to their feet.

"Lamont." Lina's voice sang loud from down the hall, beckoning him. Followed by a sick ripping sound. "Lamont." A terrible crescendo, an awful melody.

In immediate response, the house shook somewhere far below them. He hadn't pursued them into the wall, only laughed and marched off. With each step, the impact grew louder; he grew closer to them. The three looked at the gaping door. If they did not want to join Willow, they could not stay here.

"We have to find Talia," Colin whispered as he reached under each of their arms.

Another wet tear and the splat of liquid hitting the floorboards in the distance. A furious ripping and gnawing. Autumn could see Lina's tongue whipping in the air in her mind. Lamont's steady parade continued until they heard his footsteps settle on their floor.

Autumn looked to the door with its bloody path leading to the noisy feast. Colin held Ricky up on his mangled legs. She didn't wait for any suggestions. She pressed their tangle back into the wall.

The door slid back into place, restoring the wall in front of Autumn and sealing them back in the darkness. All hands went out to orient them in the black, the hall defined in touch. Ricky pulled away from her shoulder, but she could still hear his gentle sobs and sniffling breaths. She heard Colin tracing and retracing the walls.

"Thank you," Ricky said, his voice sounding wet.

"Oh, baby." Autumn reached out to find his face. He snuggled into her hand, cheeks wet and slick, for an instant.

"We cannot stay in this wall," Colin breathed.

"Where's Talia?" Ricky asked.

Autumn shook her head, though no one could see it. "We don't know."

"Is she—" Cries stole the question.

"We don't know," Autumn said again.

"We have to find her." Ricky's voice rose. The sniffles dried up, and his energy solidified in the passageway. "I let them take Willow. I won't let them take Talia."

Autumn squeezed his shoulder in solidarity.

"We'll find her," Colin said. "But not in this tunnel."

Colin seized Autumn's wrist to guide her forward. She found Ricky's and led him along. She was blind with both her arms occupied. Colin had not given her time to latch Ricky onto her shirt. She floated suspended between them, following the wobbling shape of Colin's lead.

Then Colin stopped. She bumped into him and Ricky into her, like dominos, yet Colin held fast.

A dim red light in front of Colin provided a faint shape to the passage. Autumn saw Colin's silhouette raise his hand, and she reached back to place her fingers to Ricky's lips.

Quiet.

"She was scared." Lamont's voice said from the other side. "I can taste it."

"Even more than our little lamb," Lina answered. "So tender."

With the greedy sounds sneaking under the wall, Autumn could only see two tiny ballerinas.

Steeling her throat, she clenched her jaw and screwed up her face. Colin eased back into her, and she guided Ricky back with her elbow. They retreated along their path. Colin stopped until he located the familiar seam.

"We're back to where we started," he said.

"Where do we go?" Ricky's voice jabbed at her.

The passageway felt like a tomb.

Talia felt a million miles away. These walls were keeping her from Autumn. In her bones, Autumn wanted to tear this house down with her bare hands to find her child.

"Breathe, Autumn." Colin stepped closer, his breath on her now.

She shot an arm out, colliding with his chest.

"Shhhh shhh shh," Ricky hissed beside her.

Striking out, she found Ricky's shoulder.

"Whoa, whoa." Colin took her wrist in a gentle grip. "It's okay. Let's go back to the bookcases. Ricky." He reached over Autumn and tapped Ricky, pivoting him around. "That way."

Ricky gulped. Then he shuffled down the passage.

Moving, Autumn's skin settled back over her muscles. Her throat relaxed. They could get out of the walls in that bizarre sleeping chamber. They could run and find Talia.

Ricky crept them forward. Colin's fingers dragged on the wall. Then he jerked to a stop and snatched her shirt. She snagged Ricky before he could disappear into the dark.

"Here," he said. "I can feel the seam."

Autumn turned to where the shapeless wall would be. Coming in close, Ricky took her arm. He shivered slightly against her, and his skin was wet. Blood, sweat, or whatever was in those smashed jars. A chemical smell wafted off him to form a cloud in the narrow space. Part of her wanted to shove him away and reclaim her space. The rest of her wanted to pull him close and run calming hands over his head, cradle and comfort him.

What have I done to these children? They were supposed to stay home. They were supposed to take care of Talia. Her heart sank. *I was supposed to take care of Talia.*

Grunting, Colin's mapping of the wall grew more frantic. The fingertips circled over and over, retracing the same patterns. His foot tapped in changing shapes on the floor.

"I can't find it." His flustered voice filled the hallway.

"What?" Ricky's words squeaked.

"I can feel the door, but I can't get it to open. I—"

Colin's words were shattered as a splintering impact filled the passage. Falling back against Ricky, Autumn choked on the dust. Flickering light from the chamber blazed into the dark, painting the walls and floor for her sight.

Lamont's thick arm punched through the wall, his long, pointed nails scratching for them.

TWENTY-ONE

THE VOICES ABOVE Talia vanished. As she focused and searched for them, she made out a faint scraping. It inched across the ceiling, tracing the edge of the room before turning along the next wall. She followed the sounds with her eyes. Once they slid past the kitchen, she chased them into the sitting room.

The fire had reduced to smoldering embers, glowing in a rolling red. Scorch marks branched out from the fireplace where Ricky or Willow had liberated the flames. Talia held herself as the dawn air nibbled at her from the smashed window.

The shuffling above stopped again, and the voices returned. She could not tell who was talking, but there were multiple tones. Someone was alive. More than one of them. Her heart fluttered at the possibility that she had not failed them all.

Her momentary elation was smashed with the crash above her. On the other side of the ceiling, things broke and fell, colliding with the boards. Then the screaming started.

Thoughts fled Talia. She became fear and determination. Without consideration or hesitation, she ran from the room, nearly skidding out on the turn to the stairs. She swung around the banister, splinters chewing at her palm, then barreled up. Her feet squeaked and slammed on the wood. She did not hear them. She only heard her body, shaking and panting.

"Stop fighting. Come here." Lamont's voice came from down the hall, around a corner Talia did not know.

"Colin!" Her mother. Her mother was alive. "Fuck you! Let him go. Colin!"

Fire surged from Talia's chest until her limbs crackled. Her muscles heeded instinct, forgetting exhaustion and injury. At the summit of the stairs, the red light spilled onto the floorboards. She ran faster.

As she turned and reached the door, Lina stepped from it. Blood poured over her chin and down her chest, spreading to the black lace of her dress. She held her long nails in front of her face, her tongue winding around each to slurp up every drop. Talia nearly collided with her, and Lina lowered her white eyes down to Talia, the pinpoint pupils dilating in excitement.

"Little lamb." She stepped to bar the hallway. "I didn't order another course. But I suppose I am still hungry."

Fear doused the flames in Talia. She skidded to a halt. Sneaking one foot back, she fled Lina's smile down the hall, past the red room, away from her family.

"What part of you should I try next?" Lina advanced in pace with Talia's retreat. "Every person tastes different. Your pale friend was soft and sweet, like a baby animal."

Talia gagged. She kept the images of Willow out of her head, staring into Lina's awful eyes to keep her fear sharp.

"And every part, every organ, feeds something different in us. Your young, little ovary filled me with youth. Your friend's pure liver cleaned my system."

Talia's heel bumped into a door. She gathered herself against the wood, cornered, bracing.

"You're so strong, so willful." Lina closed in on her. "Perhaps I should eat your heart, absorb all that love and courage."

Lina raised her vicious hand, tongue wavering up toward the ceiling. The claws came fast, whistling through the air. Talia could feel them slicing through space before they reached her. She threw herself against the hall wall, dodging the blow. Lina's talons grazed along her arm, parting her shirt and calling up lines of blood.

Pouncing, Talia lunged at Lina. Without thought, she snatched the slender tongue from the air, cinching her hand around it. The edge of the tongue, lined in faint spikes, bit back. Immediately, the acidic saliva burned and ate at her flesh. Talia cried out, yet held fast.

Lina gurgled, slashing at Talia. Talia bobbed out of reach, leading Lina by the tongue and circling behind her. Tongue pulled taut over her shoulder, Lina gagged. Yet she did not pull back. She followed Talia's movements.

So, it must hurt.

Talia took a brief relish in this. She even forgot the fire slicing through her hand. She held Lina, no matter how it scorched her skin, and enjoyed being the one in control.

She pulled harder.

Yanking down, she spun and brought Lina to her knees. Each time Lina struck out at her with her claws, Talia jerked the tongue in reprimand. Lina's eyes narrowed and near glowed in their hue. Talia grinned at her and wound her other hand around the tongue.

The pain doubled, but she ignored it. With Willow's name in her mouth, she gave the tongue a savage tug. A wet pop and thick rip erupted from Lina's mouth before her shriek filled the hall.

As Lina collapsed to the floor, Talia released the tongue and turned to run. The wounded muscle dangled from Lina's jaws. Talia had torn the root but had not wrenched it free. She watched Lina gather it and roll it back toward her mouth, whimpering as she cradled it.

The tongue, Talia thought. *The tongue hurts them. The tongue might be their weakness.*

Then she hurried around the corner, blind, into the next horror.

A whirlwind of Spanish screaming directed her down the hall. She rushed past the red room, avoiding its contents, knowing Willow was dismembered within. Colliding with the next wall, she turned fast and ran until she barreled through the open door.

She did not see the room. She only saw Lamont punching and tearing at the bookcase. A scatter of books carpeted the floor, pages ripped, spines broken. Her father pressed up against a pile of books, blood trickling from the side of his head. He clutched his ribs as he struggled to stand. Her mother stood behind Lamont, clawing, punching, kicking at his solid form.

Lamont was unaffected. He seized Ricky through the jagged opening. Ricky thrashed and slapped, continuing to spit Spanish curses, as Lamont extracted him. The pointed wood bit at Ricky as he passed through the wall. Lamont gathered him by the shoulders, holding him in the air, before pitching him across the room.

Ricky landed hard and limp at Talia's feet. He was there, right there. She could touch him. Throwing herself to her knees, she put her hands on his back to ride the rise and fall of his shallow breathing.

He was still alive.

Clutching Ricky, Talia looked up. Lamont's sharp tongue slid back and forth under his ghastly eyes. He raised his claws in front of his face, shorter than Lina's, but just as sharp and menacing.

Her parents had not seen her. Colin was on his feet now, joining Autumn in her futile assault. They battered the massive figure, but he swatted them away like bothersome flies. He shoved Autumn back. With the space between them, he ripped his hand down, sending his claws carving through her chest.

Autumn stumbled back on her heels a moment. Wavering in her waning balance, she looked down, slowly lifting her hands to the injury. The wide, deep slashes wept crimson. Her hands barely covered one slice. Touching them, she gazed down at her bloody palms. Her face slackened as she slammed to her knees.

"No! Mom!" Talia cried.

At the sound of her voice, Colin whipped around. Glimpsing his daughter, his face softened in fear. Lamont also took notice, smiling over his shoulder. His tongue slowed its dance and pointed to her. Colin watched him, then sprinted over to his daughter.

"Go!" he shouted. He pulled at Ricky. "Go go go."

"But Mom," Talia sobbed.

"Go!" he bellowed in her face.

Ricky roused enough to stumble along with them as they fumbled down the hall. Lamont followed them, dragging Autumn's limp body by the shoulder. His long strides chased them to the closet. The closet where Talia had hidden in before careening down to the basement.

Releasing Autumn, Lamont pounced after Colin. He cleared half the hallway and ripped Colin away from Talia and Ricky.

"Dad!" Talia yelled.

"Just go, Talia. Run!" he sputtered as Lamont pulled him back. He braced his arms against the walls, blocking Lamont from them.

Lamont seized him. His massive paws consumed Colin's shoulders and spun him around. Lifting Colin by the neck, Lamont held him in the air with his feet searching for the floor. He wriggled his claws in front of Colin, slow and teasing.

Then he tipped his head to look past Colin. Talia seized at his eye contact, at those shining white orbs. She didn't know if her heart had stopped beating or was going to explode. Lamont's flapping tongue wiggled at her. Smirking, he punched into her father's chest. His fist disappeared. Colin gurgled and coughed, collapsing over Lamont's grip. With a sick sucking sound, Lamont extracted his hand, gripping Colin's stomach, intestines chasing it out.

Talia knew that stomach was full of macaroni and cheese. Juni's favorite.

Lamont bit into the stomach, the juices pouring down his chest, as Talia and Ricky watched in horror. All the while, he stared at Talia. He released Colin to pile in a sickening heap, exhaling a satisfied breath and a wet burp. Intestines and another fleshy lump splatted on the floor. The sour, rotten smell rolled down the hall in a wave.

Before they realized it, Lina shoved them aside. They slammed into the hallway wall as she dove to the floor, stabbing a nail into the flesh and bringing it to her nose.

Reaching down, Lamont picked up Colin's limp body, leaving Lina her snack. He pitched him into the closet, down the chute, as if he were a rag-doll. Then he turned to Autumn and dragged her body to the closet, shoving it through and down.

"For later," he said, licking his lips.

TWENTY-TWO

Just go, Talia. Run!

Talia's father's words rang in her ears, but she didn't run. The world around her, the slurping sounds of Lina and Lamont ingesting her father's innards, slipped away and behind an increasing buzz in her head.

Mom. Dad. I got you killed. Once she thought it, the words looped into a chant.

Shock enveloped her. She could not even feel her body anymore. She could have been sitting in the back of the ambulance with an EMT wrapping a blanket over her shoulders for how she felt.

"Talia," Ricky called her from an impossible distance. She barely registered the sound. "Talia." Her name again. What was her name? Did she have a name with no family? "Talia! *Dios mio, chica*! Let's GO!"

Ricky's fingers dug into her arm, but she didn't react.

"For fuck's sake," Ricky grunted.

He yanked on her arm hard enough to bring her back. The sound of the hallway crashed into her like the tide, sucking her into its undertow. Lina was laughing as she ate, the sizzling of her tongue on the flesh forming a hissing symphony.

Tongue already back in action. Not that much of a weakness.

Then it all faded behind them as they hurried down the hall, back toward the stairs. Talia made it to the red light spilling onto the floorboards. Then she stopped. It pinned her in place. In its glow, she heard her own cries and imagined Willow's.

She hesitated at the threshold, forgetting the monsters behind them. Placing her hand on the doorframe, she hazarded a step forward, glancing back at Ricky. At the top of the stairs, he gaped at her, foot hovering over the step. Then his gaze found the room. The red light made his eyes glow. He staggered after her.

Willow was everywhere. She was not given the delicate surgical treatment Talia was. There had been no restraint, just unmitigated violence and hunger. Willow's head rest against the extinguished candles on the wall, thankfully with her face turned away. Her matted and tangled hair stuck to the floor. Her limbs scattered in all directions, while her torso lay hollowed out on the table, ribs reaching out like welcoming hands.

Right where Talia had lain.

Behind her, from down the hall, the monsters were distracted eating her father's stomach. The smell of the inside of him lived behind her nose as her throat tried to close against it. Distantly, she wondered what a stomach did for them. Perhaps it aided their digestion. Perhaps it would make eating her and Ricky even easier.

Ricky's jaw worked, teeth grinding and cheek flexing. "No matter what I do, I can never do right. I let her die, crawling on the floor like a bitch."

Reaching up, she pinned his lips closed with her fingers.

"We have to get out of this house." Ricky's low voice fell flat.

He said the words she had been repeating in her mind all night. She had never thought a phrase so many times. The words barely held together anymore. They slipped as syllables along the worn passage in her ears.

At the pit of her stomach, she knew there was no getting out of here.

"How?" she managed.

"The front door. They are distracted."

Talia laughed without meaning to. It all felt so pointless, so futile.

"We have to try," Ricky pressed. "I'm getting you out of here. If it's the last thing I do. I won't lose both of my girls in this fucking place."

Talia could not find the words he wanted to hear. She could only think, *I got them killed. This is all my fault. I deserve what I get.*

"Talia!" Ricky kept his voice low as he shook her. "Your parents would be furious if they saw you like this."

Rage bubbled up in her, acidic, along her throat. She wanted to yank her hand away, storm away from him.

But he was right.

They had come here to avenge her, to protect her. Now, she was dragging her feet down the stairs in resignation, trying to lie down with the pieces of their bodies. They would be so disappointed.

The dark cloud in her head cracked with lightning before clearing. She found herself again—her parents' daughter. They would not have another dead daughter, even if they were not here with her.

Whirling Ricky around, she plunged them down the staircase. They cleared the last few in a single leap. The door was right in front of them. Where it all started. The nightmare folded over on itself, placing her back on the same floorboards where she began. Where she would end it.

The doorknob was nearly in her hand when the weapon careened past her head. The axe bit deep into the wood just above her, burrowing into the door and frame, barring it shut. At the impact, Talia and Ricky separated and fell to the floor. Ricky's eyes grew so wide that Talia could see her own shocked face in them.

As Talia looked behind them, another weapon whizzed over. The long spear planted into the center of the door. It wavered and sang in the impact. Flattened on her back, Talia glared up the stairs.

Lina and Lamont were on the staircase, high enough to be veiled by shadow. Lina's arm lingered in the air an instant, a direct line to her spear, then lowered to her hip. Lamont stood on the step below, hands balled up at his sides. Though their eyes had faded back to ice blue, they were both smiling.

Talia threw herself at the door, seizing the axe handle. She yanked with all her might, ignoring her screaming hands, planting her foot in the wood for leverage. Ricky tugged at the spear, but it only wobbled. He groped at the doorknob, but the weapons held the door fast.

Behind them, Lina laughed.

They were caught. They were trapped. They always were.

TWENTY-THREE

TALIA RELEASED THE axe handle. It remained unmoved by her touch. Rolling away, she pressed her back into the door, freedom mocking her on the other side. Ricky abandoned the spear and slumped beside her, holding his ribs. The fight had drained from his face. His clothes had dried stiff and pink. Blood trickled down the side of his face as swelling blossomed under his cheek.

Lina pinched a pale lock between her normal fingers, staring down at Talia and Ricky. Lamont stayed in front of her like a sentinel. Leaning on his shoulder, the finger twirling her hair grew sharp again. The nail threatened. Talia could already feel Lina's tongue thinning and pointing toward her.

"I'm so full, Lamont," Lina whined. "Do you think we can have another course?" She glared into Talia.

"I'm sure we can make room," Lamont chuckled. "We can always eat more. Or pack it for the road."

"Oh yes, the road. It will be a long journey."

The monsters did not move, lazy in their teasing, but Talia could not stay there. She could not wait for them to saunter down the stairs and leisurely devour them. Reaching down, she yanked Ricky's arm.

It felt stupid to run, futile to limp around this house of horrors crafted into a huge trap. Where were they going? There was never any getting out. It was all over the moment Talia stumbled onto Monere Lane. Yet it was impossible to stand still and face those white eyes.

They tumbled into the receiving room across from the dining room. Curtains hung thick enough to deny the morning. In the corner, a massive, ornate clock ticked. Each second boomed, counting down, keeping time to their end. Lina and Lamont did not descend the stairs, did not bother to chase. Yet Talia could still hear Lina's constant laugh following them. Ricky grunted softly beside her as they hunched low against the wall.

Talia fumbled through the curtains, the velvet heavy and resistant. Her fingers clawed through to strum along metal bars. Metal bars bolted on the inside.

The windows were just another tease, another chuckle in Lina's throat.

As Talia's mind reeled, Lina and Lamont tromped down the stairs. Making no effort to march softly. They moved in no rush. Lamont stepped to the floor and reached his hand back to Lina. She took it and swirled around him as if they were starting a dance. Her lace skirt spun, hovering over the floor. As they passed, they kept their cold, fading eyes locked on Talia and Ricky, fixed directly above their smirks. They paraded past and proceeded down the hall, back to the sitting room.

Talia's thoughts whirred. The blocked door, the barred windows. The blood and chunks of her family haunting all floors of this house. Lina's sizzling tongue scorching her palm.

The tongue. The tongue was the weakness, the only thing that had brought the monster to her knees. But how to use it? How to get past the claws and the strength and use it?

How do we get out of here? Talia thought on repeat.

"Come on." Talia guided Ricky to his feet and hustled him across the floorboards.

She groped along the wall, even as the day brought the hall into focus. It remained dim and foreign. Shoving them past the stairs, she dove into the darkness beneath. She did not have a plan, but it felt safer tucked out of sight.

"I hid here with Willow." Ricky choked around her name. "I should have done better." He smacked at his forehead. "I always knew I would be a waste. Just like my dad and brother."

"Shut the fuck up." Talia sank her fingers into his arm until he grunted.

His groan dribbled into a soft sob.

"I have told you for years, that is a bunch of bullshit." She patted him gently. "It's even less true tonight." She turned from him and plopped her chin on her knees. "I did this to us."

"Oh, bitch." Ricky's whisper stiffened as his posture straightened. "No." The word dropped heavy on them. "None of that shit."

"From you either, then."

He glared at her through the shadows but then smirked, giving a light nod.

"I am going to look." She raised to a crouch.

"No no no." He groped after her hand.

"I'll be right back."

"Don't fucking say that." He reached for her again, then recoiled in pain, folding into the shadows.

"They're just fucking with us," she told herself aloud.

Pulling away from him, she found the hallway wall with her fingers again. Lina and Lamont's voices danced down the hall, yet she still crept. Her entire skeleton vibrated under her skin. Her muscles quaked. The entire night trembled through her.

As she reached the open door, heat radiated out. She wanted to melt into it. She would set herself on fire if it meant not feeling the way she did. Yet she rejected the warm comfort and focused. The sight of Lina and Lamont made her go cold again.

They sat together on the couch, Lina leaned onto Lamont's shoulder. Lamont dangled a piece of intestine between his hands, twirling the end in front of her so that it threw blood droplets. He giggled at his own fiendishness. Lina brought her hands to her mouth. With human fingers, she cradled and caressed a normal, fat, pink tongue, whimpering as she did it.

"That child nearly tore it out," she mumbled around her fingers. "I can't remember the last time food bit back." She glared into the flames. "I'll still be able to taste her, though."

Lamont shoved the end of the intestine in his mouth like a sausage.

Vomit swelled into Talia's mouth. Pressing a firm hand over her lips, she shuffled back, chewing and swallowing the foul mouthful. She threw herself back into the dark and clung to Ricky, adrenaline shaking through her. It took her a moment to notice the phone in Ricky's hand.

"Your phone," she gasped.

His face hung as he turned the screen toward her, exposing the spiderweb of cracks. He pressed the power button on the side, to no avail.

She wilted. Tucked against him, she drew her hands into her chest, clenching and releasing her fists to feel the tug of blistered skin.

"*Chica*," he breathed. "What happened to your hands?"

Unrolling her fingers, she offered her wounds to him, putting the scattered burns on display. Every flick of that singing tongue. A long braid of blossoming scab carved down the middle, where she had gripped tight and pulled.

Even now, feeling the ache, it was worth it. Watching Lina nurse her wound was worth it.

"I grabbed that woman's—" The words died in her mouth.

The tongue.

"What?" Ricky hissed. "You grabbed her what?"

"Tongue," Talia answered, ideas crackling over her mind. She stared off for a moment before meeting Ricky's scrutiny. "But it burned me. It hurt her, though. When I had her by the tongue, she couldn't do anything to me."

His eyes grew with each word. "What are you thinking?"

"The basement," she breathed. "There are gloves in the basement."

Besides, her parents were down in the basement waiting for them already.

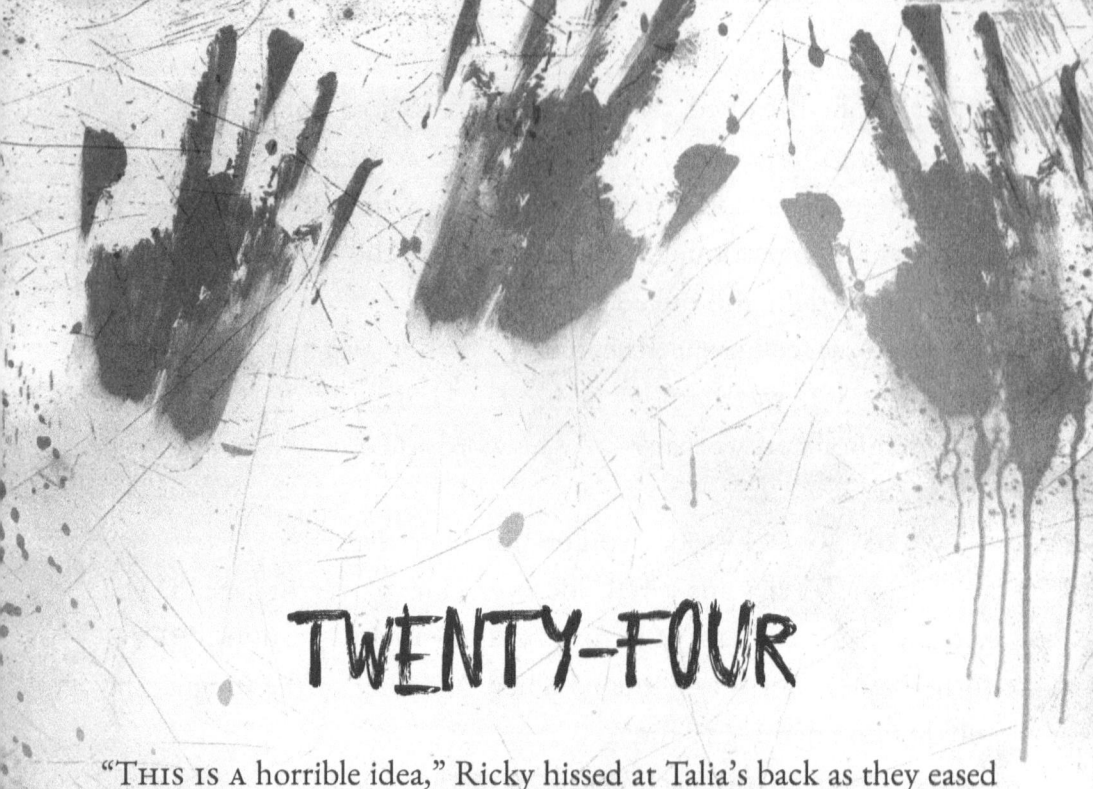

TWENTY-FOUR

"This is a horrible idea," Ricky hissed at Talia's back as they eased down the old stairs. "The basement is where you go to die."

His words floated behind them as they continued their descent. Talia trailed along the lumpy stone walls as the wet, musty smell filled her lungs. Maybe she was hunting for gloves to rip the tongues out of monster heads. Or maybe she just wanted to see what was left of her family. She could not temper her breathing—for the risk of what they would see.

"I'm happy to hear alternatives," she replied. "Would you rather we stay up there and wait to get eaten?"

The silence answered for him. Creeping down the stairs took an eternity, as opposed to plummeting from above. The basement was deeper than she realized.

When she reached the dirt, she froze. Her parents heaped, immobile, on the ground. Colin's glassy eyes found the only light in the room to glow at her. Like he was looking at her. Autumn slumped against him. Talia could not see her face, just her contorted body.

The scene in front of her eyes flickered and flashed. Her dead parents. The limp body of her sister. Back and forth, again and again. The dirt floor morphed to wet asphalt, then back again. The room was stifling, then freezing, then dank again.

Ricky took her shoulder, and she gasped, shaking tears from her eyes.

The sight erased her mind. She forgot why they were down here, what they were doing, what waited for them upstairs. Her entire family was dead. It felt like time to join them.

She bumped down the rocky face of the wall as she dropped to her knees. She didn't feel the impact. Her nerves abandoned her with her muscles, and she puddled on the floor.

Ricky stepped around her and approached the bodies. Kneeling, he straightened Colin's corpse out, rolling him to his back, extending and placing his legs. He pressed his forearm over his mouth and coughed—or maybe sobbed—before tugging Colin's shirt down and over the gaping wound of his stomach. The cloth did little to obscure the violence. Finally, Ricky rocked Colin's head in his hand, situated it, and rolled the eyelids down over the fixed orbs.

Talia could take a breath now that her father's cadaver was not staring into her. Yet she did not feel any stronger. She could not move.

Remaining in a low squat, Ricky shuffled over to Autumn. Once he got close, he froze. He gripped her shoulders and leaned in, nearly placing his ear on the body. Talia perked at his movement, rising in curiosity.

With her ears on edge, she heard it. Low sobbing, barely audible over her own breathing.

"She's breathing," Ricky said softly. "Talia, come here. She's alive!"

His words wrenched Talia from the floor. Avoiding her father's body, she hurried wide around the basement, diving on the other side of Autumn. She focused on her mother. She reached toward her with her wounded hands.

"Mom," she gurgled.

Ricky's hands moved over Autumn. Tipping her to her back, he poked and evaluated the cuts across her torso. The gashes were deep, bloody caverns, yet the organs remained within her body—behind her ribs, under her muscles. Not like Colin, with the torn end of an intestine peeking from his body, with his abdominal cavity open to the world to display his remaining organs. Talia had not paid enough attention in anatomy class. She did not know, and did not want to know, which parts of her father she could see.

Autumn's bleeding had slowed, leaving her in a pond of gore. Her breathing was shallow but steady. And her copper eyes stared through the basement wall.

Until she saw Talia.

"Baby?" Autumn's voice scraped from her throat. "Talia?"

"Mama." Tears flooded Talia's eyes as she seized her mother's hand. Autumn's skin was cool but still alive.

"I thought you were all dead." Autumn let Ricky guide her up, clinging tight to Talia.

"We thought *you* were dead," Ricky said.

The tears streamed down Talia's cheeks as she contained her sobs in shaking ribs. She did not know if she was crying in relief or grief. Perhaps both.

"I thought I was going to die here," Autumn said. "I was just going to die right here beside…"

As her words trailed off, her eyes drifted to Colin's body. Her face contorted, scrunching as if it wanted to fold in on itself. Her violent sobs could be mistaken for retching. She jerked forward as the cries escaped her pursed lips.

"No, Colin." She extended a shaking hand to him, placing it on his cheek.

As Talia watched her mother bury her face into her father's chest, careless of the carnage, she saw her wailing on that freezing night, as officers wrangled her away from Juni. Whimpering, she crawled beside Autumn and curled into her. Ricky joined in, and Autumn pulled them both in tight.

"I'm sorry," Autumn said over and over until mumbling back to soft crying.

Once they all stopped shuddering, they drew up to sit around Colin's corpse. They looked between each other's wounded faces.

"I did this to you," Autumn said to them. "To all of you."

"No, Mom, it's my fault," Talia replied.

"*Silencio*," Ricky whispered. "Both of you with this shit. It's those monsters' fault. But now what?"

Gloves.

Her mother was alive. A survival instinct rekindled in her. Hope blew on the coals.

"Is there any way out?" Autumn's face settled with her breathing.

"Everywhere we go, they are already there." Ricky wrapped around his knees.

"They are playing with us," Talia said. Lina's laugh echoed through the ceiling, as if on cue. "This is their house, their playground. We are just the latest in who knows how many. They have years, maybe even centuries, of practice. It sounds like they have been in Red Walls House itself for a long ass time."

"Centuries?" Ricky asked. "What do you think they are?"

"I don't know," Talia answered. "They have these old weapons, and there are symbols everywhere and—"

"It doesn't matter." Autumn sliced her hand through the conversation. "I don't care what they are. They are monsters. Monsters take many forms." She paused, and the words resonated. "We have to risk it."

"Risk what?" Ricky asked.

"This house is a death trap. We have to risk facing them." Talia stood and hurried over the shelves, snatching the pile of gloves in her tender grip. She dove back to them and offered the gloves. "Their tongues." She opened her palms to display the burns transecting them. "Their tongues are their weakness, but they burn. I hurt Lina."

"And yourself." Autumn gathered Talia's injuries tenderly.

"Worth it." Talia retrieved her hands, smirking at her mother.

Talia saw approval flicker in her mother's eyes.

"She cornered me upstairs," Talia said. "I grabbed her tongue and pulled. It ripped or something. Whatever I did hurt her. If we can hurt them bad enough, we can get out."

"If we can get to Monere, the city will be waking." Autumn raised an eyebrow and slid her fingers into a glove.

"They don't want to be discovered. Not before they move on to somewhere else," Talia added.

"We are not going to die here," Autumn pulled herself up from the floor. "We are not going to become part of this bullshit urban legend."

"I wish the legend would have mentioned organ-eating monsters." Ricky cradled the gloves in his bloodied hands.

The blood crusted around the hard points of the glass fragments. Talia winced at the sight and drew closer to him. She did not know if it was her hands or his limbs that were trembling.

When she glanced at him, he nodded. She tried to use the tips of her nails to pinch and push the pieces loose. Her fingers seemed so blunt and fumbling in the echo of the monsters' surgical talons. Ricky's breathing strangled, and chunks of glass pinged to the ground. Her fingers slicked with his blood.

Each time she moved her hands, he grimaced. She ignored the flares on her nerves as she concentrated on Ricky, but once all the glass—or all the glass she could see—was picked out of his flesh, her own skin commanded attention. The scorches across her hands balked and objected.

"Five people can't disappear with no one noticing." Autumn winced and cradled her gloved hands. "Your family, Willow's family will look for us."

Talia looked between them. "Figures all our hands are fucked up."

Autumn whirled but let the swear pass. She looked down at Colin, her features softening. Crawling over to kiss his bald head, she lingered, whispering against his skin. She touched his face again and again as her tears fell. Then she struggled to her feet.

"Now," Autumn said. "No point in waiting."

She limped around the body and to the stairs. Ricky whimpered as he struggled on the gloves, then hobbled after her as fast as his flesh would allow. Talia looked at them, then down to her father.

Her quiet, loving father. The family peacekeeper. She did not know how she and her mother would survive without him.

She could not touch him again, could not imprint that sensation in her memory. She wanted him alive in her mind. She wanted to remember every night before this one. It felt wrong to leave him, but it felt worse to be close to his mangled corpse. Flicking away a tear, she plunged her hands into the gloves, ignoring the flare of pain. She eased away from him, her eyes lingering until she reached the others.

They snuck up the basement stairs and filed into the hallway. Ricky clutched Talia's elbow, leading her away from her dead father and back to the monsters.

"We have to leave now." Lina's voice drifted down the hall to them. "People will notice this feast. People will search for this meat. We must return to our old ways. Vagrants, addicts, people no one will miss. I was sloppy this time, complacent from being here too long."

"Whatever you want," Lamont answered. "As always."

"At least we will be full for a while," Lina cackled. "I haven't felt this young in decades."

"We haven't fed like this since we crossed the water."

"Maybe we need to throw in a feast every now and then," Lina's voice danced.

"Maybe when we prepare to leave," he added.

"One final party."

They both laughed, and Talia's stomach turned.

Ricky squeezed both of them and led them back to the stairs. "I'll draw them out," he said. "I'll create a diversion, or whatever, and you both can run."

"That is fucking stupid," Talia snapped. "The bait always dies."

"If I don't do this, we all die, *chica*." *Chica* never sounded so sharp.

"No," Autumn said, firm and final. "I am the adult. This is my fault. I will distract them."

"No," Talia said. "We are all getting out of here."

TWENTY-FIVE

"I'M FEELING MUCH better," Lina's voice cooed.

The sound drifted down the hallway to Autumn as she glared sternly at both kids. The monster's voice alone ruffled her nerves, causing her muscles to corset around her ribs. She gathered Talia and Ricky close behind her.

She was the adult. She would face the monsters.

"Yes, it's fully healed," Lina continued. "Let's go finish our meal."

Autumn strove to keep the tremble out of her arm. They were coming. They were coming now. She flexed her pierced hand in its glove and felt completely unprepared. Yet the momma bear was also rumbling in her blood. Its growl hushed the pain climbing up so many nerves.

"What about the leftover meat?" Lamont's voice was closer to the door now.

"We can pack that up after we dispatch the rest." Lina was nearly in the hallway now. Her shadow danced on the boards in front of them.

Lamont grunted in reply.

Autumn's foot twitched to surge forward, to fling herself into the fight, but the heat of the children at her back stopped her. Instinct shuffled her along the wall, shoving Ricky and Talia around the stairs, through the dining room, and into the kitchen.

"Mom, where are we going?" Talia whispered.

Autumn didn't know what to say, so she raised her hand to silence the question. Her heart beat louder than her thoughts. She had to get these kids out of here. Lamont's steps marched down the hall in no hurry as Autumn pulled them past a dented refrigerator, blood dried along the freezer door seam.

"Do you think they went up or down?" Lamont asked.

"Down," Lina answered. "To the parents."

Autumn's chest clenched, but she kept gliding them across the floor. Talia planted her feet, yanking on her mother's sleeve. Her wide eyes and raised eyebrows asked the question for her. Autumn gestured at the far door, circling back to the hallway the monsters just vacated.

The answer solidified in her mind. The room they had left. The broken window she had made with her first ill-fated step into this house. They could get out now without ever having to grab a sizzling tongue. She could fix this. It was right there.

Listening to the heavy steps descending into the basement, she looped her arms around Talia and Ricky and spirited them out the door, across the hall, and into that first room. The rekindled fire continued to writhe over the logs in the hearth. Lamont had been stoking the flames for Lina. Yet a chill slithered through the warmth from the open window.

"The window," Talia exhaled into the realization. "Let's get the hell out of here. They're going to know we're gone."

"Wait," Ricky said. Autumn and Talia looked at him, and he turned to the fireplace. "Let's set it on fire first. Keep them busy while we get away."

Autumn nodded at Talia. "Do it fast," she urged.

Frantic, Talia searched the mantle. The fireplace tools rattled as she pawed around. Until she found the kindling and accelerant. In a basket in plain sight by her foot.

She gathered up wrinkled and soft newspaper and smaller sticks from the basket, shoving them into Ricky's arms. Then she gripped the fuel bottle. Pointing it down and spraying steadily, she drew a line from the fireplace across the room and to the door. On slow, quiet steps, she continued the path down the hallway, flicking the bottle to spread the accelerant further. Then she hurried back to the room.

"There." Talia pointed to the door. "Pile them by the door. On the fuel."

Ricky moved and dumped the kindling in front of the door. Using the large metal tongs, Talia pinched the flaming log on top. She leaned back as she lifted it and took deliberate steps toward the kindling pile. She glanced at Autumn with her wounded hands shaking, and her mother nodded.

The fire leaped to life as she placed the log on the kindling. The fuel caught and drew fiery lines across the room and down the hall. Feasting on the old wood and ancient house, the flames grew high and hungry. The three stumbled back against the blaze of heat.

Ricky stooped to the fire and ignited a small stick. "Bring the fuel," he said.

He held the stick like a candle and hurried to them. Holding the curtain back, he waved Autumn and Talia to the window. Without looking down, Talia swung her legs over and dumped herself to the ground. Autumn followed. The dead grass came up fast, compacting her legs. She did not feel it. All she felt was the outside air on her face, the impossible chance of it.

Talia stared up into the window. "Ricky," she called.

Instead of Ricky, a stream of fuel splattered over the windowsill. Ricky painted with the bottle before tossing it over his shoulder back into the room. He lifted the burning stick in front of his face before looking down at Talia.

"Ricky, what are you doing?" Talia's voice climbed. "Come on. Let's go. Get out here!"

A sad but resolute smile played on his lips. "Run, bitch," he said.

Autumn's heart stopped.

"Ricky, no!" Talia yelled. "What are you doing?"

Autumn wanted to hush her daughter, but she was rooted in inept shock. "Ricky, don't," she managed to mumble. "You don't have to."

Stepping back from the window, Ricky pressed the fire to the sill. A curtain of flame rose between them, obscuring his face.

"Run, bitch," he said again from the other side.

Talia surged toward the window, plunging her hands into the fire. Autumn dove to snatch her waist.

"No!" Talia shrieked. "Don't you fucking dare. Ricky! No bullshit bury your gays self-sacrifice. Fuck you, Ricky! Get out here! Come with us!"

Talia clawed at the windowsill through the flames until Autumn dug her feet into the dirt enough to haul her back. Her daughter shuddered in her arms. Her cries filled the breaking dawn.

"Talia, Talia," she said into her hair. "We have to go. We have to go *now*."

The flames lapped out from the window like a floating funeral pyre. They stood transfixed for a moment. They could not hear Ricky. No screams. Nothing.

TWENTY-SIX

Ricky watched the fire consume the curtains until he could no longer make out Talia and Autumn below. They almost looked safe on the other side, the fire like a screen between the house and the outside world.

Run, bitch, he urged in his mind as he swiped away the springing tears.

He wished there was another way, any alternative. The monsters would have never let them run down the hill. They had no chance of running away together.

And he was so tired. More tired than he was after long days of his smiling theatrics. More tired than he was after classes and clubs and volunteering and work and caring for his mother and younger siblings. He was tired, the way he was alone in his room, those final seconds before he collapsed into sleep when he wondered if he should just stop bothering.

His body throbbed, begging him to heed the pain coursing through him. He was exhausted from this night, and if he was honest with himself, every day before this.

Sloughing off the gloves, he let them fall to the floor.

As he forced his steps toward the kitchen, fear and tension replaced fatigue and pain. Icy waves swelled and receded along his skin, making him sensitive enough to feel the air around him. A vice clamped around his lungs and reduced his capacity to breathe. He gulped shallow at the air, like he was struggling to keep his head out of the water.

Something else rose from the fear. In that twitching terror, apprehension flitted through his veins, pumping urges into his brain.

You're going to die, he told himself. *There is nothing after this. You are giving it all up. Anything you would have been or done.*

When he thought about the life he was abandoning, saw his mother's face, thought of college, a hole opened within him, deep enough to swallow him. That same abyss he looked into before he fell asleep alone. His thoughts could scarcely form enough to quantify it.

Nothing after this.

Yet the clicking montage in his brain settled on Willow and Talia. His chosen sisters. He was losing them tonight either way.

You're saving them. You're giving them a chance. You can do better right now and run out before you have the chance to fuck it up.

He staked his mind on these ideas, the tremble in his conviction wobbling into resolve. Shaking his hands, he fought his sore body to walk strong and tall, fire spreading through the house behind him.

Then a darker voice, the part of him he tried to squelch, spoke up. *None of us are going to survive this, anyway.*

The kitchen was painted gray and grim in the morning light. It looked like a lifeless model of a kitchen, sterile and unused. Aside from the bloody refrigerator.

His family lived in the kitchen. His mother presided over the family from that stained linoleum. Always preparing a large meal full of colors, aromas, and flavors. They congregated there, worshipping their own dynamic. Serious talks and impactful decisions were solidified on those counters, at that table. His mother had told them their father had left in that room. They had decided to send his brother to rehab in that room. He had found out about his unexpected sister in that room. His mother told him there was no need to come out, that she had always known and loved him in that room.

This room looked like a dead husk of what it should be.

Ripping open the cabinets, he gauged the empty shelves. A few glasses. No plates, no bowls. Nothing like the metal goblets in the other room. Sighing, he shrugged only to himself. Then he struck across the shelf and sent the glasses shattering on the clean tile.

The sound of the glass made him wince. It reverberated through his knees, his elbows, his palms as if it were beckoning shards still implanted in him. The noise also crashed through the silent house. He caught himself flinching and fought the impulse to hide.

No more hiding. No more running.

As he ripped open drawers and sent knives clattering beside the glass, he imagined getting into UCLA. And in the same breath, he saw himself washing out, finding the heroin that had killed his father. Another inhale and he was kissing a tall, muscled boy amid the throb and lights of a club. Then he saw himself alone in a shitty apartment, the only single son returning for holiday dinner. The possibilities flickered through him.

No pots, no pans, no serving dishes. He turned to the fridge and pulled it open. Immediately, he recoiled. He did not know what exactly he was looking at, but he knew they were human pieces. A fridge and freezer full of packaged human organs. Like all those shelves and jars he had crashed through. He nearly vomited, then smiled.

The grin felt sick on his cheeks. But he felt sick everywhere.

He hesitated, then plunged his hands into the fridge. His fingers pressed into the flesh of the first bag, the meat bobbling in its own liquids. A feast made of an unimaginable number of unwilling donors. Winding his arm back, he flung the organ at the floor. It landed with a satisfying splat, the bag splitting to splash the contents over the mess he had already made.

He could not contain the laugh as he grabbed another bag, maybe a set of lungs, and chucked it into the window. The organ flattened before bursting free of the container and raining down over the sink. The lungs draped over the faucet, unfurling to their full shape.

He reached in again and again, heaving the bags across the room, tossing them over his shoulder. Steadily, a bloody lake rose at his feet. He shied away from how euphoric and manic he felt, how satisfying it was to rob them of their food.

If he still had Willow's heart, he would shove it down their throats, past those scalding tongues and rows of teeth, until they choked.

"What do we have here?" Lina said, propping an arm in the doorframe.

Ricky looked up from the center of the blood pool, unapologetic and vindictive. Lina turned to Lamont, raising an eyebrow.

Lamont crossed his arms over his swelled chest and shrugged at her. "It is a wise tactic, destroying the enemy's food supply."

Lina smirked and nodded. Her icy eyes moved to Ricky. "You couldn't think you could escape, did you?"

"He's not trying to escape." Lamont's hand wound into his beard. "He is a sacrifice to save the others."

Lina raised her eyebrows, pursing her lips. "So, he has chosen Valhalla." Her smirk melted to a soft smile, eyebrows relaxing. "Brave."

"Indeed."

They both turned to Ricky. He remained frozen in his crimson lake, his mind reeling at their words. He was not brave; he was terrified, more scared than he thought he ever could be.

Before he could react, Lina snatched him by the neck. However, she held him loose and plucked him from the blood, guiding him to them. Lamont closed in so that his odor was in Ricky's nose and chest was at his back.

Lina looked Ricky over, through him, to Lamont. "We should turn him."

At her words, Ricky's mind ignited with panic. He squirmed in her grip, but she flexed her hand to encourage him to calm.

"You have never turned one before." Lamont's voice pinched.

"Except you."

"Yet no one after."

Lamont's hot breath grew heavier on Ricky's neck. Ricky leaned away from them, but Lina squeezed his windpipe.

No no no no no. Not one of them was all Ricky could think.

"There has never been one like him." Lina glanced at Ricky, her eyes growing paler for an instant. "There have been no other warriors. All before were food."

A frustrated grunt escaped Lamont.

"You could have been food too, long ago." Lina narrowed her eyes at Lamont. "But you were a warrior, and I chose you."

"And now you choose him too." Lamont's voice deflated.

"No!" Ricky forced out through Lina's grip. "I'm not like you. I'm not one of you."

Lina smirked at him as one would look at an ignorant and misbehaving child. "We need another. A modern warrior who has no old memories and is a child of this time. He can help us develop new strategies and camouflage better."

Ricky's chest tightened hard enough to push his heart into his stomach. Every cell in his body screamed objections.

"Fine," Lamont said. "Let me turn him. You promised to teach me."

Lina shook her head, blood-tipped blonde locks swinging at her shoulders. "Not this one." Before Lamont could object. "You are *my* warriors. I will show you how it is done."

Another angry plume washed over Ricky before Lamont acquiesced and stepped back. "I get to turn the next one," Lamont said.

"If there ever is a next." Lina flicked her wrist. Turning, she pressed Ricky into the wall. "Fetch him his first meal." She jerked her head at Lamont. "The one in the basement has plenty of meat left. He has not been dead long."

Lamont marched in a subdued tantrum, his steps pounding harder to the basement and back. He kept his eyes down as he extended a slab of flesh to Lina, blood spilling from his hand to join the red ocean at their feet.

"A kidney." She grinned as she looked it over, forcing Lamont to continue offering it. "Perfect choice to cleanse him of his former life." She ran a tender hand along Lamont's beard before turning to Ricky. "Now, hold still, my new little warrior. This won't hurt. Much."

"No no no no no." The word dribbled from Ricky's lips until they were squelched by Lina's severe turn of his neck. The wall pressed into his cheek to gather his distressed, helpless tears.

This is not what I expected, he managed to think.

Lina moved her hand from his throat and palmed his skull into the wall. His body flailed in desperate resistance, but she did not even notice. Her nails extended around his scalp, tips flirting with the wall. From the corner of his eye, he saw her irises disappear into white, black pupils dilating in excitement. Her gray tongue unspooled past the vicious rows of teeth.

Leaning in, she plunged that tongue into his ear. It sizzled past the lobe and burned through the narrow cavity. He felt the piercing pain dig through him. Until the tongue licked his brain. Fire blazed through his skull, engulfing him in a cacophony of sensation. His nerves went electric, from his brain down every branch of his nervous system.

Lina released him to slouch on the wall, retracting her tongue. He remained immobile, frozen by the current of tingles coursing through him.

"Yes, warrior," she cooed into the cavern carved by her tongue. "Time for your first meal."

Slicing a corner from the kidney with her talons, she shoved the chunk into his mouth, blood dripping down his chin.

TWENTY-SEVEN

TALIA FOUGHT AGAINST her mother's embrace until the tears overtook her. Her fingertips blossomed in blisters, and her nails cracked from the heat. None of it mattered with Ricky still in that house.

She hated him for his dramatic exit. He would have it no other way, and she didn't know how to imagine a life without him. Or her father. Or Willow.

But her mother was there, clinging to her, bleeding on her.

They couldn't waste this chance. They had to get out of here.

Autumn turned Talia away from the Red Walls House as the flames crackled inside, and all trace of Ricky was lost behind them.

Talia's mind kept raging, kept screaming. Her consciousness stepped out of her head to linger at that window, to shriek after Ricky as her flesh mechanically followed her mother into the woods.

The trees cradled them. Talia passed her mother to navigate over rocks and underbrush, now tragically familiar to her. She chased the echo of herself trying to escape those monsters in the dark, the house blazing brighter than the sun behind them. Their twisted shadows jumped on the rocks and trees ahead of them. From the corner of her eye, Talia saw her hiding tree and hoped the fire would spread wide enough to swallow it and its memory.

Monere Lane looked close, close enough for them to clip their pace and stumble in their hurry. Talia was never going to be on this street again. Not driving, not walking. She would never see that asphalt line to hell again.

When her feet hit the street, Talia sagged into her mother. Avoiding the gashes on her chest, Talia clung to her and breathed in the sour, smoky odor of the night from her skin. As they embraced, a car rolled up beside them. They released each other and turned to regard it.

"Devon?" Talia scrunched her face and stepped back from her mother.

"Who?" Autumn placed a hand on her hip.

Talia squinted at Devon through the windshield, then moved to the passenger side. He lowered the window as she crouched down. His bloodshot eyes swam above a lax expression. Even when he tried to react, there was a winch at the edges.

"Talia, what are you doing here?" He leaned over the center console to her, and she could smell the stale beer. "Where did you go?"

"Long story." She stood and waved her mother over. "Can you give us a ride?"

"Sure, of course."

Talia ripped the passenger door open, waving her mother to the backseat. They dropped into the car and clicked their seatbelts fast.

"Okay, where to?" Devon slid the car back into drive and brought his foot off the brake. "Yo, did you see Red Walls House is on fire?"

TWENTY-EIGHT

THE FRONT DOOR cracked as Lamont tugged the axe from it. In a swift pull, he yanked the door open and from its hinges. Pitching it back into the flames, he stepped aside for Lina to exit. Then he stomped in front of Ricky to follow her.

Ricky coughed as he stumbled from the porch. The flames chased him as they consumed the house, rolling from the center out the windows and up around the roof. Moving beside Lina and Lamont, he followed their gaze. Down in the distance, he could make out Talia and Autumn diving into a car. Something familiar, but now distant, twitched in his chest.

"Awww, they did not come back for you." Lina stuck out a pouty lip then smiled.

The world pulsated around Ricky. The sky felt close; the ground felt far. The contrast had been turned up on his ears and eyes. His sight was crisp, and his ears tickled at every sound as if they belonged to him. As he flexed his muscles, he could feel their lean strength. An impulse to run seized him. He knew he would be fast now. Nothing hurt. The injuries from the night seemed like a distant memory, like they had happened in a past life.

"Look at the lambs run," Lina laughed.

As he gaped around the new world, Ricky's sight paled, except for the three red forms speeding away down Monere Lane. His dark irises faded before dissolving into white. His pupils expanded, and he could make out the shape of Talia, down to the braids in her hair.

A thick crack came from his hands. When he looked down, his fingers twitched and snapped in ways a finger should never be able to move. He observed in calm detachment. Nothing hurt. The nails sprouted from his fingertips, sharp and severe. Lifting them in front of his face, he waggled them in amusement. The old him always enjoyed a manicure.

Pressure spread through his jaw. When he looked over to Lina, she dropped her mouth open and tapped behind her teeth. A second set of teeth sprouted through the roof and floor of his mouth, piercing through the soft tissue with no resistance.

Then his tongue grew small in his mouth, receding away from those new teeth. It thinned and elongated in a tough line. The barbs on the side tickled at his lips. It did not burn him. He saw it as it climbed into the air in front of his white eyes.

"You cannot return to your old life." Lina turned to him, her face serious. "They left you for dead. They will know, and then all will know about us." She paused and glanced down the hill. "You cannot have that life back, but you will live a hundred lives with us."

"It was nice of them to set the fire." Lamont looked to the flaming top of the structure. "We were leaving anyway."

"They did a good job of cleaning up our overindulgence," Lina agreed.

"Gave their dead a proper funeral." Lamont's laugh was clumsy.

"Now, we just need to tie up the loose ends. Before they tell anyone else." Lina lifted her chin to Ricky. "Are you ready for your next meal, your first real feast?"

Ricky said nothing, just waved his pointed tongue.

Lina turned back to the road. "Goodbye, little lamb," she said, as her eyes went white.

Drawn to the monstrous and macabre, Christina Bergling has been weaving nightmares since childhood. Her horror tales slither from post-apocalyptic (*Savages*, *Screechers*) to monsters (*Red Walls*) to psychological (*The Waning*) to comedy (*The Rest Will Come*) to mystery (*Followers*) and anything in between (various anthologies and zines including *The Horror Collection* series, *96th of October*, *Graveyard Girls*, *Demonic Wildlife*).

Bergling is a member of the Horror Writers Association and Denver Horror Collective and a dedicated voice in the horror genre. She has been featured on panels at Colorado Festival of Horror. She devours horror in all its forms--movies, books, festivals, conventions, stores, haunted attractions.

By day, she navigates the shadows of the IT world. By night, she turns trauma into art. When she's not writing, she hikes rugged Colorado trails, dances wildly, and sucks out all the marrow of life.

THANK YOU!

Your purchase helped support an indie author and a small press.
We hope you enjoy enough to leave a review!

Want more Dead Fox books? Head on over to our website
, where you can purchase our titles and our partner titles cheaper than
you'll find them anywhere else.

www.deadfoxpub.com